I0549005

ALL THAT'S LEFT OF YESTERDAY

TALES OF THE APOCALYPSE

Edited by

A. W. Gifford &
Jennifer L. Gifford

Dark Opus Press
P.O. Box 811
Ortonville, MI 48462

www.betenoiremagazine.com

All That's Left of Yesterday is published by Dark Opus Press a division of Charm Noir Omnimedia P.O Box 811 Ortonville, MI 48462

This anthology is a work of fiction. Names, characters, places, and scenarios are the products of the authors' imagination. Any resemblance to actual persons living or dead, places, or events is purely coincidental.

ISBN-13: 978-0692367353
ISBN-10: 0692367357

CONTENTS

INTRODUCTION

Nowhere does a culture bare its soul more than in its written tales and folklore. Its beliefs and philosophies are often buried in the narratives revolving around creation and death. Societies put a religious theme to their own mythos, and over the centuries the topic of the apocalypse has changed into a multitude of facades with one common factor: a cataclysmic event that threatens that world into a chaotic upheaval.

Zombies, aliens, biblical second comings, technological meltdowns, ecological disasters, and global warfare are just a few of the backdrops for apocalyptic fiction, the scattered elements of humanity rising from the digital safe haven into a new world void of rules and social conformity. But what is the lure of apocalyptic fiction? Is it a need to strip ourselves of the material and technical garbage and restore our moral compass? Or is it a need to get back to the simplicity of life, and make our existence and the lives of those around us more meaningful? There is no great consensus of conclusion, just a wealth of stories to contemplate.

A subgenre of science fiction, the love of apocalyptic fiction grew increasingly popular after World War II, when the introduction of nuclear conflict and its devastating effects were introduced into modern warfare. Yet apocalyptic literature was common long before the nineteen forties. Babylonian and Judean cultures have mythology involving the end of the world and humanity. From the story of Gilgamesh, Noah's Ark, the Book of Revelation to the ecological floods in Sura 17 of the Quran, these fables go into great lengths about vengeful gods and human suffering as a way to cleanse humanity.

Whether it's a single protagonist or a hand full of survivors, these characters take the reader through a process of stages — disbelief, fear, agitation, hopelessness, violence, and rebirth — as humanity struggles to rebuild itself in the aftermath of a fallen society. While most apocalyptic fiction follows a similar pattern of literary structure following the catastrophic event that leads to the inevitable social collapse, there is a profound and often over-looked lesson, easily missed against the graphic narration: appreciation and endurance. Appreciation for the precious gift of life, depicted in stark contrast against the dystopian shambles of apocalyptic world. And allowing life to survive means to endure the hardships that come after the epic breakdown of life before humanity's fall, and enduring whatever dark and unnatural situation is necessary to ensure that life survives.

Dystopian views in literature often reflect the social and political upheaval from the authors own world, and is it any wonder that the dark tales of a world free of the social static and background noise is appealing? The need for escape into a hellish civilization teetering on the ashes of its former self is psychologically comforting, providing a temporary escape which allows us to realize that our actual reality, isn't really all that bad.

—Jennifer L. Gifford
January, 2015

ALIEN ANIMAL

BRANDON L. SUMMERS

Donnie raced through the ruins of the city, leaping over concrete and dodging rusted frames as the wind howled through the hollowed buildings. The destruction had only bothered him the first year. It had since become the new normal, and the past a dream. All he cared about now was getting back to the bunker with the package he had pressed against his chest.

He panted in a crumbling factory, struggling to take deep breaths and reduce the amount of noise he made. It could hear them, he knew, and probably even see them when they were in the city, but the thing's motives were elusive. Maybe even mad.

He wiped the sweat from his brow, and then his hand on his tattered blue-grey jumpsuit.

"Come on, Marty. Where are you?" He was afraid. An hour was pushing it, and they had been in the city for almost two. "Please. Don't make me leave you behind."

He bounced in place, waiting. And then he heard it. It was distant, like a whisper, the electronic trilling of its flying robotic agents.

With a sharp intake of air, he ran.

Donnie charged through the shadows, from one building to the next, toward the bright light in the distance. He jumped into it then, springing out onto the torrid brown wasteland.

Now, he was really afraid. The luxury of cover he enjoyed in the city was gone. Under the intense vanilla-white sky, he could be spotted easily. He held back nothing, finding the strength and speed he had honed from a decade of necessary raids.

After a while he began to tire and slowed. He glanced back. The city was a small thing in the distance. There was something else, though. It was growing larger, nearing fast. His eyes widened. He didn't have to think. He knew what it was. And even though he doubted he had a chance, he ran for his life and nothing less.

No! Why now? he thought. *I've never been caught before. Never! Oh, God! They were counting on me!*

Donnie looked back, but it wasn't there. As the hot wind blew over him, he glanced up. It had bounded and was soaring through the air, aimed right at him. He staggered and fell watching it, and the lank, hairy creature landed over him with a thud.

The man shook as he waited for death, dust rising over him still, but the hunched beast did nothing. He opened his eyes, stared at his reflection in the dark glass of its round goggles. Its head was wrapped in a crimson shroud, hiding a breathing apparatus, though he could hear its harsh wheeze.

With a soft, high voice, it said, "Do you wonder what happened to your fellow hu-man? Watch!"

The creature brought its fists down then, and for Donnie everything went dark.

ଓଃ

In the obscured bunker, miles away, Alice worked diligently on a device the size of a television remote control, the sonic disruptor. With it, they could create a nullifying field that would make them invisible to the flying robots and allow them to move more freely, maybe even locate other survivors. It only needed a final component. Everything else was refinement.

She stopped twisting the micro-screwdriver to push a lock of her blonde hair behind her ear. She couldn't wait for Donnie to return from the city. They needed fresh supplies, of course, but mostly she worried about her little brother, just as she did when they were kids. And she couldn't endure being apart from Martin. Her lover was her sole reason to keep going. These rare days being alone approximated her nightmares.

"Martin," she muttered, resting her weary head in her hand. "Hurry back to me, please. I'm dying without you. Can't you feel it?"

The young woman stood, stepped around the worn wood table. A single bare bulb illuminated the otherwise empty concrete room. She walked into the hall. It was quiet, its shadows cool. She ran her hands down her faded pink shirt to her green cargo pants—a habit from before the world was destroyed—and continued forward.

There were three rooms ahead, all at her right. At the end of the hall, a metal door, excessively reinforced, led outside, but it was not a way out.

Alice entered the first room, and sat on the edge of its bunk. She looked over Jimmy. The nine-year-old jerked in his sleep, moaning softly. She pitied every minute of his life. His head was swollen, his brain damage an effect of being conceived in a poisoned world. They had to keep him drugged, or he would wail and holler without end. And they could not take the chance of attracting their single enemy.

Alice pushed her fist into her leg. They had only seen it in vague images captured on corrupted digital video. But they knew its intentions, and gave the monster a name.

"Ape-Man. That...alien animal," she muttered. "You deserve a better world than this, Jimmy."

She put a hand on his arm. He seemed to calm, and even smiled. The sight broke her heart. She lay at his side and held him. The boy squirmed warmly against her.

"When I was your age," she said, "there were fields of grass as far as you could see. And flowers of every color. It was so, so beautiful. I would run in the grass all day, and pick the flowers and put them in my hair. I was happy, but I was too young to appreciate it. That's how it should have been for you." She kissed the boy's head. "I love you, Jimmy. We all love you."

She stood and started to leave. From the threshold she glanced back, hoping again that his dreams were filled only with happiness.

Alice went into the next room less eagerly. Here, her grandfather, Mylo, sat in a chair in the corner, so white-gray he glowed in the shadows. He looked up weakly at her, and smiled.

"Taking a break, are you?" he said.

She grit her teeth. He had meant it innocently, but to her it was a stern admonishment.

"All it needs is a stronger capacitor, and Martin said he'd get one from the city. It should be done tonight."

Mylo raised a bony finger, and pointed it at her.

"It's only a matter of time," he said. "Others will come. We were not eradicated out of whimsy. No! Minds capable of such magnificent evil, they must have some plan for our world. And it requires our death."

"I know," Alice said. He said it every time they spoke and usually not much else. And still, she visited him. "You taught me well. Everything. They will be gone soon, and we can live again."

Mylo shook his head. A tear ran down his cheek. "Oh, Alice. Sweet Alice," he said. "This is all our doing. We dedicated ourselves to suspicion and fear, and turned our hatred toward one another. What we must have looked like to our attacker. Mere petty children. And now, you suffer for my mistakes."

Alice looked away. Mylo had been one of the greatest minds of his time. He inspired her to follow his path. Now, she hated him. She already blamed him for their misery and resented him for dying so slowly.

Her frustration only lasted a moment, though, before she remembered who their true enemy was, and what still had to be done.

"Try to get some rest," she said as she left.

In the hall, Alice leaned against the concrete wall. She looked longingly at the metal door, wishing they would return. Nothing happened, though, and with a sigh she headed back to her workstation to resume her lonely, tiring perfections.

The device worked, according to various tests, but its connectors, circuits, even the simple button that activated it, could never be perfect in her eyes.

She remembered the blinding flash when she was twelve, and the deafening rumble that lasted for days. After it had calmed and the light diminished, they emerged to discover the city had been incinerated. The atmosphere had exploded, unleashing solar radiation upon the world in a single burst, and then instantly repaired itself. It announced the arrival of the robots, and their master.

The bunker had been their salvation. Mylo began work on the disruptor, with Alice serving as his protégé. Donnie became the errand boy, and on one of his trips found Martin wondering the wasteland, seeking survivors. Alice fell in love with the man, and Martin with her. Their hopes of restarting the human race, romantic when she was sixteen, were shattered when she birthed Jimmy. Despite what Martin said, she blamed herself.

Even if the device worked, she knew their lives would never get any better than this.

Alice reached for the case at the end of the worktable and lifted its lid. She often looked at the thick black cylinder inside, a frequency amplifier, and considered the possibility. Mylo had made it two years after the invasion, as the continental military was finally scattered. It used the robots' wireless network to reach across the world and activate every nuclear warhead, untouched and undiscovered still by the invaders.

It was a last resort, a promise if she ever failed.

BOOM!

Something thudded hard against the metal door. Alice gasped, stopped her work as she looked up. Its echo faded, leaving only stark silence.

She trembled, waiting. It could be anything. They used a specific knock when they returned, one they all knew. But there was only the single thud. One of them could be hurt. There was no other noise, though. It could be their enemy, testing them. But, why now?

She got up, crossed the length of the hall.

"Donnie?" she finally said. "Martin? Is that you?"

There was no response.

She opened the door. The hot wind and intense white light washed over her. She looked into the concrete pit, and what she saw made her scream.

"Oh, GOD! Donnie!" she cried. "No! NO!"

Her brother's head rested on the dusty ground. Alice looked beyond the horizontal slit of the sunken bunker, her eyes filled with tears, but saw no one else.

"I'm sorry!" she shouted, and slammed the door closed. She fell against it, crying into her hands. "I'm so sorry!"

An hour passed before she found the strength to open the door again, collect Donnie's head and bring it in. She couldn't look at it, already struggling to remember him. Their lives were miserable, but they'd had each other. He always had a cheery attitude.

What was it he would say?

Alice went into the room she shared with Martin, a subconscious act. Finally, she looked down. Donnie's face was twisted in horror, made more severe from being exposed to the heat. She only hoped he hadn't suffered too greatly, that Ape-Man had been merciful.

Then, she noticed something. She angled the head under the room's bare bulb. Donnie's mouth was slightly open, and there was something inside. It was a metal orb, silver and perforated. She jolted, but quickly realized it wasn't a bomb or some other weapon.

It was a speaker.

She leaned toward it. "It's you, isn't it?"

For a long moment, there was only silence. Then, a deafening burst of static.

"Hu-mans ..."

Alice shuddered. She had never heard its voice before, couldn't even imagine it. It was very human, soft and calm and, almost, beautiful.

She bravely responded, "Yes. This is Alice."

"You are the female," it said. "I want to meet you."

"Why?" she shouted. A lifetime of quieted rage welled inside her. "You know we're here! Why don't you just come after us? Why don't you kill us, the way you ... the way you killed Donnie?" she sobbed.

A pause. "You are the female hu-man," it said. "Come into the city. I will find you."

With a final burst of static, silence returned.

Alice knew she had no choice. She had to go. Jimmy was still asleep, and Mylo would never notice her absence. The food, medicine and parts they needed were still out there, too. And she had to find Martin.

She covered herself in a sheet, and as an afterthought collected the frequency amplifier from the workroom. It was her only weapon. She used a magnetic key to seal the bunker behind her, and then set across the wasteland.

It had been years since she was last outside. Nothing had changed. The sky was the same blazing white, and the earth still scorched. More than once, she spotted a black-purple lizard in the distance. They were twice as large as the lizards of her youth, and calcified and poisonous, the product of accelerated evolution.

The city appeared in the distance, a hazy blur on the horizon, and soon she was standing among its ruins. The stories Donnie and Martin told her after they returned from their trips had made this place familiar to her. And still, it filled her with wonder.

Alice kept alert, but after three miles hadn't seen or heard anything, not the flying robots or the monster.

She stopped, and took a breath amid the wreckage and overgrowth. She considered shouting out to her lover, but feared it would draw the Ape-Man to her. It must already know she was here, she thought. And she realized that, for the first time in her life, she was not afraid of it. She didn't believe it wanted to kill her. It could have done so at any time, and hadn't so far. What did it want then?

"Where are you?" she muttered. "OW!"

Something had bit her. Alice clapped her hand to her mouth, staggering back as she looked down. It was a black lizard. It hissed, sprinted back into the rubble.

"Oh, no! Oh ..."

She suddenly became dizzy, lost all her strength and collapsed. She lay on the ground, shivering and gagging, like she was drowning in a frozen lake.

A shadow fell over her then. She looked up, the effort a painful one. Someone was approaching.

A man.

"Martin?" she cooed.

It shuffled nearer and stood over her. The sun gleamed off its dark goggles as it wheezed mechanically, gaunt and covered in orange-brown hair.

"Ape-Man ..."

Its hands reached out as the blackness enveloped her. Her scream was a whisper that existed only in her mind.

☙

Alice groaned as she awoke, feeling weak and sore all over. An icy chill caressed her. She tried to raise her arms, but they jerked, tugged in place. Her eyes opened and she gasped, discovering she had been bound to a chair and stripped naked. As the haze lifted, she could clearly see the bold, dotted marks covering her body. She screamed and thrashed against her bonds.

They were surgical marks.

What does it want? She thought, already tiring. *What is it going to do to me?*

Alice calmed, and searched around her. The vast space was cool and musty. Ahead, there were several long tables, one covered with outmoded electronic equipment, buzzing and grinding. Another, occupied by beakers filled with chemicals of various colors, bubbling over flame and noxious. The floor was littered with bones and shreds of rotting meat. Its putrescence filled her nose and made her shudder. She willed herself to ignore it.

Beyond the tables were five tall mirrors in a crescent configuration, each spotted with filth and slightly fogged. And in the distant shadows were stone columns.

I'm under one of the buildings, somewhere in the city still. I must be, she thought. *So, it doesn't live in the sky.*

Alice heard something then, a dull *thump* in rhythm with an electronic wheeze. She had heard it before, in recordings over the years and earlier, as she was passing out.

It loped past her, powerful stink wafting from its hairy body. It stopped ahead, and after a moment turned. She stared at it in awe, forgetting her horror and years of hate. No one had ever gotten such a good luck at the thing and lived to share the details. Its veins glowed green, and its body was riddled with raw sores.

It was not a primate, as they had always thought, but she wasn't entirely sure it was alien.

"What are you?" she asked.

Ape-Man looked down as it raised its hands, and then glanced up at her. Even though a crimson shroud and goggles covered its face, it clearly expressed confusion.

"They made me," it said.

Its ghostly voice unnerved her in the close space.

"I don't understand."

"They made me," it repeated. "I am like you."

"You're human? Oh, God!"

"God?" it said. "That does not compute." It turned away, uncertain and panicking. "I must make my report!"

Ape-Man ambled to the second mirror from the right, and stiffened at the sight of its reflection.

"Great Leader Two," it said. "I have succeeded in capturing the female hu-man."

It paused. And Alice watched as it responded to itself with an entirely different voice.

"You will examine the female," it said, its tone dark and angry. "And when you are done, you will annihilate the hu-man."

It responded softly, "Understood, Great Leader."

Ape-Man turned and shambled back then, picking up the long serrated knife on the steel table along the way. Its gaze fixed on her.

Alice, struggling to remain calm despite everything, hoped even a small part of its fragmented mind was capable of reason.

"You can't do this. Not yet," she said, her tone firm. "Not before you tell me what you did with Martin."

Ape-Man halted, showing its confusion again. Without a word, it set down the knife and began darting from one dark niche to another, rummaging through the garbage for reasons she did not want to fathom.

She spotted it then, on the corner of the far table. The frequency amplifier! She knew she couldn't really use it. But, if she could get free, maybe she could use it to scare the monster away and escape.

Ape-Man picked up something then, something large, and hefted it before her.

"Here is your hu-man male. Here is Marr-TON."

Alice whimpered, and then screamed. The animal held the ravaged, disarticulated body of the only man she had ever loved.

"Why? Why did you do it?" she shouted, weeping. "Why did you have to kill him?"

"The hu-man frustrated me!" it exclaimed. It threw the corpse onto a mound of expended chrome equipment, creating a terrible clatter. "It refused to share needed information with me! And so it served no purpose."

Tears streaked freely from Alice's eyes. She couldn't even remember the last thing she'd said to him.

"You're a monster."

"They made me! I must obey!" it said. "What the hu-man would not relinquish, I took. I removed its brain, and in its electro-chemical coding I learned of your hidden base. I saw you. And experienced emotion."

She sobbed. "I loved him."

"Love? Love-love-love-love," it stuttered, unable to process the word. "Do I love? I love ... you."

Alice looked up at him. "How can you love?" she spat.

"What I did not consume, I used!"

Ape-Man threw back its arms and thrust out its chest. Its hairs parted, revealing a stitched, bright red wound.

"You replaced your own heart?" Alice said, horrified by the sight. "But, that's impossible!"

"The hu-man male's strange emotions have corrupted my mind!" it shouted. "Love! Desire! LUST! I am supposed to be logical! Why did you have to come here? Did you not see the warnings? There is danger!"

"What danger?"

"There is ME!" It screamed in agony at her. "I love you, Alice! I LOVE YOU!"

Ape-Man stomped around as it roared, kicking the bones and broken trinkets on the floor. It turned over a table, its components falling to the ground noisily, sparks flying from the shattered contraptions.

It grabbed a femur then, charged at Alice and bashed her face. She wailed, the pain blinding. The monster stared at her with utter fascination, breathing hard and clutching the bone no less tightly. Blood oozed dark from her mouth. She coughed hard, and a tooth flew out.

Ape-Man reached for her, but hesitated, and ripped its hand away in disgust.

"I have these emotions, but this body feels nothing! What is it to feel?" it asked. "A response to stimulation? Another emotion! Nothing! Nothing! Why does it elude me?" It neared her, an inch from her face now. "Do you have a smell?"

Alice quaked, refusing to meet its gaze. The monster growled, then turned and threw the bone in frustration. The femur struck the center mirror, shattering it.

Ape-Man raised its hands to its mouth, and howled in anguish, "NO!"

It raced away, looked over the shards and then cowered before the other mirrors.

"Report! Report! Great Leader has been obliterated!" it shouted. "Wrong! This is all wrong!" It stopped then, and in a low register said, "The loss of Great Leader Three must be rectified. Kill the hu-man now! You must!"

Alice tugged at her bonds. Then, she heard it. A faint tear. Hope. She hid her smile as she gripped the straps and began rubbing their fabric against the jagged undersides of the metal chair.

"But, Great Leader. I cannot," Ape-Man said to its own reflection. "I cannot!"

It responded, "You must! And you will! Use your hands! This is an order!"

Ape-Man turned then, and stalked toward Alice.

It growled darkly, "And all orders must be obeyed."

"You're insane!" she shouted.

It extended its hands, ready to grip her throat, but stopped. It convulsed harshly, visibly fighting against its own programming.

"Must! Cannot! MUST! CANNOT!"

Alice kept going, feeling the bonds become slack. And finally, they snapped. She sprang from the chair, punching both her fists into Ape-Man's chest. The monster roared as it fell back. She collected the amplifier and ran, dodging the stone columns as she disappeared into the dark. A red light appeared in the closing distance. She hurried toward it and found a narrow hall.

Ape-Man scrambled off the floor, chased after her.

"There is no escape from me!" it shouted, its voice echoing around her. "FOOL HU-MAN! THERE IS NO ESCAPE!"

Alice ran down the corridor, up the stairs at its end, and into the light beyond the threshold. She sprinted past the bare mannequins and metal racks, unable to escape the animal's frantic screaming. She leaped through the vacated display window, emerging naked onto the street.

She searched, panting, knowing she couldn't stop, but unsure where she was or which direction to take. It didn't matter, she realized. Every direction took her further away from the monster. Before she could take a step, though, she heard a shrill beeping and electronic hum behind her.

"No!"

Alice turned. It was a shining silver disc, one of the Ape-Man's flying robots. The vertical stripe of black glass on its side faced her, studying her.

It twisted several degrees then, and fired a shrieking beam of red light that whizzed past her. She yelped, jolted as she looked back.

Ape-Man stood behind her, one hand over a smoldering, gushing hole in its chest. It looked ahead at her, reached longingly for her, and then collapsed.

Martin, she thought, fleetingly.

Alice faced the robot, and waited.

"Do not fear," it said, its digitized voice soothing. "We are here to help. Are there others like you?"

She nodded, immense relief surging through her.

"Yes! Oh, God! I thought we were the only ones!" she said, breathless. "There are two more of us in a bunker, out there, in the desert. My grandfather and my...my son. That thing, it killed the rest of my family."

"Do not fear," it repeated. "Do not fear."

Alice winced, struck by a grim realization. Dozens of robots swept from the sky and down the street in a shining blur, heading in what could only be the direction of their bunker.

"It's you," she said. "You're the invaders. You're the ones who destroyed our world. All this time it was you, not the Ape-Man."

"Ape-Man, as you have designated it, is our creation. Its purpose was to find hidden clutches of surviving humans and destroy them. You are the last female human. Once you are dead, your race will cease to be a threat to us. Thus, Ape-Man no longer served a purpose."

"It was trying to protect me from you."

Alice raised the device clutched tightly in her hand. She never thought it would be used. There had always been some hope that humanity would rise as one and defeat their enemy, the roving monster. The robots, though, numbered in the millions.

"Am I truly the last?"

"Yes," it affirmed. "Do not fear."

Alice gazed at the robot, and wondered what the alien attackers looked like, if they took a physical form or were an electronic intelligence existing unseen in the digital ether. That she would never know the answer did not bother her, she discovered.

Donnie was dead. Mylo was near death. Jimmy never had a chance to live. And the man she loved was dead, twice. The rest of the world had died ages ago. There was no hope. There was nothing.

"I tried," she said. "I really tried."

Alice exhaled, smiled. And activated the frequency amplifier.

For days after, there was a vociferous roar. And for months longer, white brightness enveloped the world. When some semblance of dark finally returned, all that remained was the scarred earth and its inheritors, the lizards.

ೞ

Brandon L. Summers *learned how to write by self-publishing short novels until he figured it out. During the day, he is a reporter for a daily newspaper in Iowa.*

THE BOOK

MATTHEW ANDREW

The old man pulls the bolt of his rifle back and checks to make sure brass shows inside the carbon-dusted chamber. The boys are out again, bruised and muddy and huddled around a crucified corpse.

The old man, trudging home with his dog along the creek after a morning hunt, watches from the edge of the pine forest where he spies the group of boys in the field under an umbrella of wet, leaden sky. The biggest one of the bunch pokes the decayed body with a hickory switch. They stand in their own little violent Golgotha and stare up in silence at the dead.

The old man is bottlenecked into the field by the creek and a converging stream. He steps into the clearing. The greying shepherd sprouts an angry mohawk along his back and growls at the gang.

Laughs cracked in puberty echo through the expanse while the boys desecrate the asexual husk that hangs from the timber crossbeams. The old man skirts the tree line behind them and the dog follows. A dead squirrel, trussed to a thong that hangs from his belt, thumps against his thigh and his wet, worn boots emit a leathery creak with each hurried step.

Crows perch on the corpse's shoulder and squabble over the flaps of skin that hang from its cheeks. Dried lips are pulled back over its teeth in a stiff grin. A wood placard hangs around its neck, with dripping red characters of condemnation that pronounce: *TRAYTER.*

A small boy whacks at the torso and the feeding black birds scatter, squawking down at the bunch. A bigger kid in a bowler hat cuffs the little boy in the head and sends him sprawling. He looks down at him and laughs.

A twig snaps under the dog's foot and the boys all turn their heads like one malevolent organism. The kid in the bowler grins, gap-toothed with his freckled face, and lobs a rock the size of a grapefruit. It smacks into mud next to the old man and the dog stops to bare his teeth.

The boys laugh and throw more rocks that rain down around the old man. A fat, round-faced one pulls a switchblade from inside his tattered, dusty vest and opens the shiny blade with a metallic *snik*.

The old man levels the rifle and pulls the trigger from the hip, sending a bullwhip crack over their heads that reverberates through the field and scatters the boys like the crows before them. The man and his dog trot across the field into the tree line. He hears a stampede of footsteps pursuing them and summons more speed from his dry, twisted limbs.

Curses and laughs from behind them. Rocks snap branches in mid-flight and the debris falls around the fleeing hunter. The dog turns and barks.

C'mon, dog, says the old man. They scamper through the dense foliage and disappear under the dark canopy while the jeers and yells fade behind them. The dog bounds ahead and then slows, leap-frogging to wait for his master while they negotiate trails only trodden under by their own six feet.

The old man slows to a walk when the only sounds are his ragged breathing and stomping footfalls. His arthritic hip screams and twists a hitch into his gait.

"I just might hafta shoot one next time," he says to his dog.

☙

He stops at an outcropping to monitor the approaching darkness.

The old man sets his rifle against a twisted elm and pushes a homemade plug of tobacco into his cheek with nicotine-stained fingers. He leans on bent knee, boot heel resting in the divot he's eroded over several lonely decades, and regards the distant purge bonfires through binoculars. Thin lines of smoke drift from behind intervening hills and merge into a gray mass that dims the sun and adds a chill to the autumnal wind blowing through the valley.

The old man scans the basin below. A dirt road veers off the hardball and leads to a lone manse—a colonial hemmed in by dry fields—and then meanders into the empty hills.

Gusts of wind slam a loose screen door and spin the creaky tin rooster perched on the peak of the faded barn. A little girl sits on a porch rocking chair and brushes a doll's hair, her own auburn wisps fluttering in the wind, while a handsome woman with matching hair in a bun hangs white linen on a drooping line. The woman's mouth is moving in song and she pulls wooden clothespins from the pockets of her gingham housedress for the corner of each sheet.

The dog nudges his leg.

"Knock it off," the old man says. "I'm comin'."

He lays his rifle over his shoulder. The dog follows him up the broken trail to their refuge.

☙

The old man walks up to his cabin along a plank he keeps laid out in the dirt to bridge spring muds.

Jeb's on the porch in one of the maple rocking chairs. He taps both knees with wrinkled, bent hands and his chin quivers while chewing on gums long absent of teeth.

The old man leans his rifle against the railing next to Jeb's gnarled cane and eases into a matching chair next to him. The dog lies down at his master's feet.

"Mornin', says Jeb.

"Didja know crucifixion was used by the Romans to humiliate slaves and enemies of the state," says the old man. He picks up a rusted coffee can and rocks his chair in tandem with Jeb.

Jeb swats the air. "You and yer damn books," he says. He holds one nostril shut and blows a gob of snot into a red handkerchief. "Went into Candler today," he says. "Talked to Mae at the shop."

"Uh-huh," says the old man.

"Seems them search gangs aren't just doin' random sweeps," says Jeb. "Seems they's doin' a...what did she call 'em?" He scratches his stubbly chin and the porch creaks while he rocks. "*Purging*...that's it," he says. "*Purging* of the county. District governor's ordered summary execution or transfer to re-education camps for anyone obstructin'."

He turns his head and spits.

"Hm," says the old man. "Suppose I better get some readin' in."

Jeb stops rocking and looks at him. "Did ya not hear me?" he says.

The old man spits a brown string of chew into the can and stares ahead.

Jeb rocks again and sighs. "Fine. Pick your poison," he says. "Those god-awful gangs of boys runnin' loose or strangers strolling right into your house and tellin' you how to live. Or worse."

"And Fred?" the old man asks. "Did Mae mention Fred?"

"Yep," Jeb says. "He's scared. Seems he's joined up with the gangs. She didn't seem to want t' talk about it. Things is getting' bad down there, but a quiet kind of bad. Folks smile and nod and say mornin' but you can smell the stinky fear comin' outta their pores."

"Hm," says the old man. "Well, we're *all* scared," he says, and then spits. "You need some water before ya go?"

"No, thank ya," says Jeb. He grimaces and struggles to his feet, liver-spotted hands pushing on both knees. "Damn my eyes and this *gaht-damn* chill," he says.

The old man hands Jeb his knotted walking stick and follows him down the plank and out on to the gravel track. The dog pads out and stands next to the old man. They look into the gray distance. Jeb's cane shakes and his chin quivers.

"They'll be up here tomorrow. Two days, tops," Jeb says. He looks into the old man's gray eyes. "You cain't hide from everything," he says. "You ain't got no choice this time."

The old man looks at the horizon, tongue pushing the chew around in his cheek.

"I'm packing up and heading down to Maggie's over in Five-mile," says Jeb. "Things are quieter down there in Rockland County. I'll be leaving the morning after next. Feel free to join me. I don't care if you hafta bring those gaht-damn books a' yours, too."

"We'll see," says the old man.

"Well, okay, then."

The old man watches Jeb do his stooped, three-legged stagger up to the creek.

He turns and waves his fist at the old man. "What would Mary've thought of ya now, you stubborn bastard," he yells.

The old man stares down at his feet and spits.

Jeb turns and shuffles along the edge of the creek bed and disappears over a rise of tall, waving grass.

ﻼ

The old man walks into the dry thicket behind his cabin. A deep hole is burrowed under the ancient, tentacular roots of a magnolia. A moist, fertile halo of green lines the dark hole, and then fades into the prickly, scorched crabgrass and dandelions of the surrounding landscape.

He crouches and knocks away a thin layer of loam and stones and dead clumps of grass that conceals the rope tied around the base of a dogwood. He pulls the guy-line and hoists the bulging cache out of the hole. The stained blue tarp he retrieves is pulled taut by the enclosed bundle of corners, spines, and edges.

The old man pulls out one book and pushes the rest of the bundle back into the gaping maw dug under the roots. The old man returns to his porch rocker, dog following at his heels.

The book is a somber gray and bordered with a thin, faded line of gold leaf. Its canvass edges expose cardboard that's puffy from the moisture and each corner is bent like a sad dog's ears. He opens the stiff book slowly and the spine cracks before it gives way and spills open to release the pleasant musty scent of dry browned pages, paper that smells of the old town library.

A forgotten picture flutters out of the book. The old man catches it and runs his fingers over the scalloped edge of the sepia photograph. A young man grins from that same porch rocker, an expression that renders his face as that of a stranger, but there's no mistaking the woman next to him. She sits in the other rocker; long auburn locks and a hand on her belly. Her smile, wide, tipped with crescent dimples, is what won over the boy one spring day long ago.

They both just sit there, happy and ignorant. The old man wouldn't say they were better days — but they were less frightening.

The old man replaces the picture between the front cover and the first page and sees the girl's looping script —

For my husband
Love, Mary

A chilly gust penetrates his flannel coat. He takes the book inside and stokes a few logs with a poker in the black kettle stove. He sits down before the warmth and reads while the white disk of sun reaches its apex and then slips down behind the mountains coloring the horizon like a receding flame.

The old man takes in each page by lamplight. He sighs, remembers, grieves, fears, and he even chuckles, a foreign sound he hasn't uttered since his wife died in that cabin, with the infant boy following the next day.

He finishes his reading and his thinking while a newborn sun crowns the eastern peaks. The dog snores on the rug by the fire. The old man unwraps salted bacon from butcher paper, cracks open the rest of the brown eggs, and over the kettle stove he fries the last breakfast he'll eat in this bleak country.

Cঞ

From his perch he scans the scattered purge fires that have crept closer. The puffs of dirty smoke are sooty, drifting cotton balls against a wet, gunmetal haze.

Flatbed Osh-Kosh trucks and dusty government sedans are parked in the yard of the colonial home. Men in stained blue coveralls, some with cowboy hats or baseball caps, file in and out of the house, like a trail of ants, dumping cardboard boxes and armloads of books, magazines, and newspapers into a smoking pile in the road in front of the house.

One man chews a cigar and surveys the bustle with his hands on his hips. He's a mix of accountant and bandito—dress clothes and fedora, without the tie and jacket and the sleeves rolled up, with a bandolier of shotgun shells slung across his barrel chest.

One of the search gang men taps the boss on the shoulder and points up to the second floor. The old man raises the figure-eight view of the binos up to one of the dormer windows. The woman of the house, hair tussled, struggles with several men in coveralls.

Her husband rushes into view wielding an ax handle.

A *pop* and flash and the man drops. His wife kicks and lashes out at the men around her while she's dragged out of the room.

In the yard, the line of drones continues to and fro, adding more belongings to the pile, some adding chunks of wood and twigs to the growing, shimmering pyre. The screen door swings open.

The man of the house is dragged out, a dripping, brick-red stain across the thigh of his khaki trousers, men in blue coveralls restraining him by his arms and legs.

The boss man points to the fire with his shotgun held out in one hand.

The man of the house is kicking, screaming, but held down while his wrists and ankles are tied around a beam of wood like a trussed pig.

The woman of the house is dragged out next.

The boss man points to one of the trucks, cigar wedged between two of his fingers.

She's screaming and clawing at the dirt and reaching toward her husband, then thrown into the back of a truck. Two men get in with her and hold her down while the truck reverses out of the grass and putters down the dirt road back toward town and during the entire scene of eviction the woman is screaming and reaching toward her house, gingham dress and apron fluttering in the wind.

Her husband is thrashing against the wooden post. Several of the gang pick up the ends of the post, hoist it onto their shoulders, and carry it to the bonfire. The rest of the men assemble in a half circle around the flames, silent and awaiting the procession. He's laid across the fire and his screams rise in pitch while his skin chars and smokes.

The man's agony carries across the valley for what seems hours, but finally his death is done. The air is thick with a smell akin to smoked pork and kerosene.

A khaki Studebaker pulls into the yard. A man in shirtsleeves and a blond woman in high heels and business suit step out. The boss man walks over and shakes their hands. They speak in a huddle, the boss gesturing toward the house and the smoking conflagration. He walks away and the new couple unloads their suitcases from the trunk. The blonde woman points at the house and smiles, speaking to her man with her arm intertwined in his while they walk past the line of hanging sheets and then up to the porch.

The little girl stands there clutching her doll and staring at the purge fires with puffy eyes and red face. The blonde woman leans down and speaks to the girl and the girl shakes her head. The woman pulls her by the arm into the house, still smiling with her blood-red painted lips. The girl stands firm and keeps her feet planted, but the woman yanks harder and they disappear into the girl's house.

The sun hasn't yet reached its noon height. The old man wonders if the family had the opportunity for one last breakfast together, or if they knew last night when they laid down for bed that their end was near.

He sighs. He lowers his double-barreled shotgun off of his shoulder and sits beneath a projection of shade from an escarpment that looms over them. His dog curls up next to him in the shadows.

The old man pulls the gray book from the chest pocket of his overalls and the photograph slips out into his lap.

Sepia-toned smiles. He remembers how she even smiled while she held his hand and the life slipped out of her on that bloody table long ago.

The old man figures they're about done down there, but he'll wait until dark, just in case.

Until then, he reads.

ↂ

A bone-colored moon hangs overhead. Still early, but he wants the little girl to have a head start.

A black halo in the dirt road is all that remains of the family's purge. There's movement backlit in the kitchen, a shape moving over the sink, all other windows dark. He walks up to the porch, dry grass crunching under his boots. Frogs croak and crickets chirp from beyond the fields in the marshy land beyond the woods. The old man takes his boots off and leaves them on the grass.

"Stay," he whispers to the dog.

Muffled creaks under his socks while he ascends the porch steps.

He grasps the handle and presses the latch down. The trusting door of an unlocked country home yields and opens in oiled silence.

The old man slinks through the foyer toward the only light still on, a soft glow from the kitchen. The grandfather clock's slim pendulum ticks, but coupled with the old man's rapid heartbeat of a trespasser, the back and forth *clicks* sound like a sledge hammering stakes into wood. Shuffling feet and cabinet doors creaking are the only other sounds in the sleeping house.

The old man, crouched, rounds the corner into the light of the dim electric bulb.

The blonde woman, wearing one of the lady's gingham dresses—he'd seen her in that dress in town before—searches the cabinets with her back to him. A board settles and pops under the old man's weight.

"Tea's almost done," she says. "Just looking for the sugar. I'll fix all this tomorrow."

The kettle whistles over a circle of blue flame.

"Where the hell does that woman keep the sugar?" she whispers.

The oiled metallic *snick* of the shotgun's double hammers being cocked and she freezes.

The woman turns, eyebrows knitted and mouth open. Her eyes widen.

The tea kettle whistles and the old man boils, seeing her in that dress that's not hers in a kitchen that's not hers, her and her perfectly coiffed blonde bob, with her blood-red lipstick.

Her eyes dart to the side.

A cleaver gleams on the butcher block next to her.

He pulls one trigger and the boom echoes through the kitchen.

She's knocked back against the oven and is trying to hold herself up on the stovetop with her elbows and she looks at him, shocked expression carved on her dying face and blond bangs knocked loose into her eyes. Thick gouts of blood leave a trail down the oven door and the polished enamel squeaks behind her weight while she drops to the floor. Her wide eyes look through him and her mouth works like she wants to say something while she holds red hands over her torn stomach.

A *crack* from behind the old man and a white-hot punch through his arm spins him around and he fires at a figure on the stairs.

A man with a snub-nosed revolver and bed-mussed hair crashes back against the wall and leaves a dripping trail of rust-red on the striped wallpaper while he stumbles down the steps, clutching his throat.

The old man breaks down his shotgun and reloads two cartridges, keeping an eye on the twitching bundle that crashed at the foot of the stairs. Warm blood spreads along the sleeve of his flannel shirt. He snaps the breach back in place and inches toward the man, both hammers back.

The old man stands over him, looking into the younger man's huge saucer eyes. Tiny buckshot holes in his throat release an expanding pool of black onto the wood floor. He's trying to clamp a palm around his life's blood and his last breaths rattle in his throat. His bare feet work against the floor, spinning him in a half circle, smearing more blood across the hardwood. He slows and then stills, eyes glazed.

The whistling kettle finally sputters and dies as it boils over.

A creak at the top of the stairs behind him.

The little girl stands at the top, auburn hair knotted from her pillow and she's draped in a clean white nightgown. She grips a stuffed animal around its neck, tight to her chest.

The old man tells her to go get dressed and put some things in a knapsack.

His arm throbs now that the adrenaline has petered out. He sits down on the bottom step. His dog is whimpering outside the front door. "It's all right, dog, settle it," he yells. "Hold on."

The young man's blood has emptied into a pool across most of the foyer by the time the girl re-emerges. She walks down to him in her jeans and moccasins, and clutches the doll under her serape. A faded denim knapsack hangs on her back.

The old man guides her around the pool of blood. He doesn't try to shield her eyes. He figures she needs to see what the world has wrought down upon her.

☙

He holds the girl's hand and his shotgun hangs loose in the other while they walk away from her house down the dirt road.

"I've seen you at the market before," says the little girl.

"Is that right," says the old man.

They leave the dirt road and venture into the path to the old man's ridge. The moon lights their way. An owl in the distance asks questions.

Outside the cabin, he stops and kneels in front of the girl, grimacing and holding the back of his arm.

"This is as far as I go," he says. "Do ya know a man named Jeb, even older than me?"

She nods. "I've seen him before, too," she says.

"The dog will help you get up to his shack," he says. "He's leaving this place for good, off to somewhere else." He brushes a strand of hair from her eyes. "That old coot could use some company," he says.

"You're not comin'?"

"No. That old fool will try to get me to stay if I go up there. Do you know how to read, young lady," he asks.

She nods. "Mostly," she says, "just not really big words."

He pulls the gray book out of the denim chest pocket.

"Take this with you and read it as many times as ya can," he says. "I'm sure yer folks would want you to. It'll show you that not everything in this world is so bad. Ya hear me?"

She nods. He takes the picture out and puts it back in his pocket. He turns her around and secures the book in the top of her knapsack.

"C'mere, dog," he yells.

The dog pads up, purple tongue lolling and tail wagging.

"The dog'll go with you," he says. "Just walk up to the creek and follow it uphill until you see an old rusted tractor. That's Jeb's place, hear?"

"Yessir," she says, looking up at the old man.

"Go on, now. Before you get a chill out here."

The girl walks to the creek. The dog stays, panting, looking up at the old man.

"Go on," he yells. "Git."

The girl's standing at the creek now, waiting for the dog.

The old man pushes the dog away with the toe of his boot and the dog whimpers. "Go on," he yells louder.

He throws a rock at the dog. The dog jumps back a few steps but stays. The old man throws another rock.

"Go on, dog," he says. "Take 'er to Jeb's, boy."

The dog runs to the girl, tail down.

The little girl and the dog wander up the creek bed, both looking back at the old man. He hears her say, c'mon, boy, and they both disappear into the moonlight over the hill of rustling grass.

The old man heads up to his cabin to get ready.

☙

He watches them approach from the slit between two curtains.

A hesitant orange morning sun peeks out over the search gang trucks that crawl up the steep trail to the old man's cabin. They park side-by-side in his yard and one rusted pick-up snaps the plank he used to walk over the mud.

He fires a slug from an open window and the driver's head of the nearest truck is turned into a red mess dusted in bits of glass. The boss man and his gang jump from their trucks and take cover behind their open doors with pistols drawn.

The boss chomps on his cigar and looks around. He yells at some of the men to loop around to the right and hit the front porch. He shuffles in a crouch around the back of a truck in his dangling bandolier and fedora. He peeks around the back end to watch the assault but the old man's second shot opens his neck and sends him onto the ground while his blood empties and mixes black with the soil beneath.

The old man crawls behind the front door and waits for it to burst open. He pulls the picture from his pocket and lays it down beside him, sepia-toned smiles looking up at him. The stench of kerosene he dumped throughout the cabin makes him light-headed and the voices of several men yelling outside are comingled into one frantic conversation.

Stomping boots and whispers behind the door. He picks up a pistol in one hand and a tarnished lighter in the other and hopes someone on another horizon will see the inferno of his cabin and not be afraid.

Ↄ

Matt Andrew *is a former U.S. Marine who works in the banking sector in Dallas. His fiction can also be read in* Pantheon Magazine, Plan B Magazine, *and the upcoming* State of Horror: North Carolina *anthology.*

ANTIDISESTABLISHMENTARIANISM

BRANDON CRACRAFT

"It's the longest word in the English language," the doll said, the mechanism in his cheeks curling his lips into a cartoonish smile that engulfed half of his face. He put his hands into the pockets of his sailor suit. He squinted his lifeless eyes in attempt to show pride in himself.

The boy was the last human child on the block, possibly the last in the city. No one had children the old fashioned way. It was considered irresponsible. Human children were loud, obnoxious, and could be born with all kinds of strange diseases. More than once, his birth parents pretended like he belonged to someone else.

If it wasn't against the law, the human boy would've given the doll an actual name. Unlike other dolls, he was distinctly male. Most of them changed genders depending on their The Parents' moods.

"I just don't understand why you keep saying it," the human boy said. "It's kind of annoying."

The human boy's parents named him Sean, but he didn't use it anymore. Names were for adults, people that proved that they were important to the Economy. Since he was only twelve years old, he was as useless to the Economy as the homeless.

"Have you ever met a doll that knew the word?" the doll replied. His eyelid closed with a strange click. He was trying to master the wink. The poor doll had no idea how disturbing that looked. "I learned a word that only the humans use. One day, I'm going to be useful. I won't just be kept in my room all day and trotted out whenever The Mother and The Father want to show me off." He started to skip. A prerecorded giggle, the same laugh all dolls had, escaped the mechanism in his throat. "I used the word in a sentence."

"What does it mean?" the human boy said. He remembered hearing that the word was one of the longest, but no longer the longest, in the verbal database.

The doll stopped and the smile clamped down to a grimace. "I don't really know. I think it's something about god. I'm pretty sure I used it correctly. 'The antidisestablishmentarianism of god allowed our country to focus on The Economy and finally become prosperous.'" The boy's face was unreadable, and the doll started to play with the tie on his shirt. "Do you think I used it wrong?"

"Do you think the world is ending?" the human boy asked. He ran his hands through his curly black hair. His parents had darker skin that the boy's, but they criticized the boy for having hair that was too ethnic and a body that was far too short and skinny. He felt like the walking embodiment of everything that the media said was wrong with human children.

Dolls looked perfect. Human children were always born gawky. They couldn't even properly take to improvement surgeries until their late teen years.

"People have stopped having children," the human boy continued. "Everyone just wants dolls now." A doll modeled after his mother's favorite celebrity walked by, pushing a second doll in a stroller. "Sometimes, I hate them."

The doll's head turned toward the human he considered a friend. The doll couldn't express hurt. The mechanisms wouldn't allow him too. He widened his eyes and crossed his perfectly shaped arms.

"You're different," the human boy said, hoping that was enough.

The two of them walked in silence for a while. Every once in a while, the doll started to skip or the lights in his cheeks turned his face vermillion. The Parents that ordered him were playing with the remote control. They often did. The only time that The Parents wanted people to notice a doll was when other people were saying how cute they were.

"Do you think The Parents love their dolls?" the doll asked. "Do you think The Mother and The Father love me?" He knew the answer. The Parents forgot him more than once. He went a solid year without seeing them. At least, they gave him a new body to reflect the twelve years he lived with them. "Do you think The Mother and The Father even like me? They are always shutting off my vocal cords when I am at home. The Father says that he does not like it when I ask so many questions. They compared me to a human child."

The doll was gorgeous, but he looked nothing like The Parents. He had summer blond hair that never got messed up regardless of how nasty the wind got. He was thin but muscular, standing exactly one foot shorter than The Father. His parents owned several china faced dolls, and they dressed him like the perfect Victorian boy.

Something went wrong with the bundle of circuits and mass of switches that made up the doll's brain. He developed Pinocchio syndrome. The human boy was pretty certain that The Parents were going to have the doll deactivated sooner or later. It really wasn't his business. Children and the useless were never supposed to question the will of adults. They might as well question The Economy.

He was designed to be attractive to The Parents, but this doll walked differently. The doll slumped around in attempt to mimic his human friend's gait. He refused to wear dresses or the wig of ringlets. Although he would never say it out loud, he actually gave himself a name. He was named Yves. He found the name in a book and never met a human with that name.

The world morphed around the two walking figures. It recognized the human and ignored the dolls. It was time for the news. According to the human's parents, it was very important that they always watch the news. Those that were blessed by The Economy were the model for others to better serve The Economy.

As usual, it talked about all the celebrities that got new dolls. The actress showed off the thirteenth dolls she and her football playing husband recently bought. This one was painted indigo. The newest fashion were dolls that didn't mimic human colors. None of them had any particular gender.

"It's wrong to pretend that the dolls have gender," the actress explained, ordering her dolls to remain completely still except for identical smiles and periodic exclamations of *I love The Mother.* "If someone has a male or female doll, I know that they are being used for sexual purposes."

"No one thinks that about you," the human boy assured the doll, trying not to blush. He started thinking about sex, at least his body did. His boyhood sometimes prepped itself at night like he expected some phantom lover to visit him. Two nights ago, the cameras in the bathrooms caught his member enlarging. His parents put him in a device for his own good. It gave him a weird walk, but he couldn't touch himself even if he wanted to.

"I am weird," the doll finally admitted.

The human boy put his hand over the doll's mouth, even though that wouldn't silence the gears. The news were reporting all the major purchases of the celebrities. This was the most important part. He began to salivate over a pair of pajamas that all the artificially young celebrities were wearing. They actually looked comfortable, and he knew that there would be a pair waiting for him in his bedroom. His parents were good to The Economy so The Economy rewarded them.

"It's just a weird word," the human boy said when the news was finally over. "You shouldn't use it anymore."

There was silence between the two boys and then finally. "All right," the doll said. "You're the human. I should obey you." Even though his face never changed vocalization beyond the sing-song cadence that The Parents enjoyed, the human boy still felt the resentment of the doll's words.

The human boy felt awful. He wondered if he should get some of the brain surgeries his mother got. His mother used to get sick all the time. She said that it was something called "stress." The only thing that the human boy knew about stress is that The Doctors cured the condition. His mother was always happy now. Nothing ever bothered her. She was now happy to work extra hours whenever The Economy demanded. She would never ask for a raise again. That kind of thinking didn't help the economy.

Fear rushed over the human boy, another failing of being a human. He shook his father's hand the other day. He was rejuvenated to look nineteen, twenty years shaven from him. The hand felt plastic. The human boy hoped his father never hugged him again.

He shook his head. "I'm sorry," he said. "I've just got a lot on my mind. I don't have a problem with the word. It's a good word. I don't think the adults want to hear a doll use big words."

"Please talk to me," the doll said.

The human boy let out a sigh and played with one of the strands and buckles on his short pants. "I was just wondering about something," he said. "I begged my parents and they let me quit school. I can get a job, probably in one of the factories."

"Are you sure you are ready?" the doll said. This time, it was his fault that the blush mechanism went off. "I am sorry. I know that I forget myself with you. I just hear stories about people dying in the factory." He blinked twice. "I mean, I understand you wanting to obey the will of The Economy. I just hope that the factories do not kill you."

The human boy felt his testicles shrink despite the device that kept him from experiencing sexual desires. His entire body actually shook. The doll stared at him, confused and hoping that he didn't do anything to cause such a reaction.

"I'm not going to die in the factories," the human boy said, hopefully sounding more confident than he felt. "I will serve The Economy well, and it will reward me. I will become a foreman."

The doll realized that he would no longer be able to play with his friend. His head sunk in his attempt to show regret. "I shall miss you."

The human boy shook his head and forced the glassy eyes to look at him. "I was wondering I could buy you from The Parents."

"You wish to be The Father?" the doll was genuinely shocked and truly wished there was a way to show the boy how touched and confused he felt.

"I just don't want to lose you," the human boy said, realizing there was only way to make the doll understand. "I am worried about your parents deactivating you. You don't act like other dolls. I know that The Parents bought two more dolls."

"They do not love me." The doll felt anger, and his teeth ground together. He spent every moment of his twelve years trying to please The Parents.

"Would you like to live with me?" the human said, surprised at how nervous he felt and sounded. "Do you like me?"

The doll nodded, trying not to notice the homeless woman being shot by the police. There were rumors that the police were going to target the useless, repurpose them into something useful for the Economy. The Mother and The Father told the doll that it was a good idea, so the doll realized that his feelings were wrong.

"I would be happy with you," the doll said. The Pinocchio syndrome took full affect. For a second, he actually felt like a human. Not just a human, but a useful human.

A bullet shattered the human boy's spine. He fell onto the ground, and the doll performed a forbidden action. The doll stood in the way of police fire. Bullets riddled his plastic body and destroyed several mechanisms underneath the fake skin. The doll couldn't stop giggling as he fell backwards. A female police officer in full armor walked over and casually shot the boy in the head.

"That's the last of the useless," she reported. "We will be visiting the home of a shop keeper on Thirty-Fifth Street. They are also harboring a useless." She went over and sliced off the dolls head and smashed it with her weighted boot. "I also destroyed a malfunctioning doll. Let The Parents know that the Economy will replace it."

❧

Brandon Cracraft *lives in the historic district of Tucson, Arizona with his boyfriend and son. His short stories have appeared in several anthologies including* The Touch of the Sea, Night Gypsy, *and* Under the Knife. *His novel,* Family Values, *is available in electronic and paperback format.*

WHISPER MOTHER SHADOW

T. FOX DUNHAM

"Are they really made of whispers?" Tilda asked.

"All the whispers that ever were. The secrets told that broke confidence. All the *I love you*s that were never meant." Father shut the lead shutters over the remaining window in Tilda's room, sealed the valve then pulled the drapes. He checked the walls for holes. Sometimes the invaders came and poured their bodies along the plaster, seeking cracks eroded by the wind and rain.

"Where did they come from?" she asked, following their nightly routine—the stories that settled her into sleep. He tightened the ropes of her bed then pulled up the wool blanket. They hadn't enough wood cut for the fireplace. Father could only cut from the edges of the forest. The shadows slept in the deeper darkness where the shade gathered and sheltered the fleeting night. Clouds accumulated on sky, and he returned to their cottage with an armful of twigs. The weather of the later autumn chilled the house, and she shivered under her thin blanket.

"The dark of the heart," he said.

"Where do they go?" she asked.

"Into the light of the heart, poisoning it. Keep them out. Seal the cracks. Shut the shutters. And stay out of the dark." He kissed her forehead and rubbed the bristles of his shaved head along her cheek. She hated having her head shaved, but it helped keep them free of lice and other critters. Mother used to brush her red curls and forbade him from snipping with the snipers. "Are you thinking about her?" he asked.

"Can she ever come back?"

"Mom is gone."

"Why won't the shadow people let her come home? What if we told them we needed her?" They took everyone. The Whisperers ate all the cities and towns. They took them all in one night when they came out of the sky.

"I don't think it works like that," Father said.

"I want her to come home."

"Good night, love," he said. "I'll check on you in a few." Father returned to the parlor of the cabin. He never slept at night and waited until the sun began to rise before shutting his eyes. The sun always rose to drive the shadow people back into the midnight places, though some days it rained, which they needed to water their tomatoes and cabbage and peas. On rainy days, they hid inside and watched any shadows, ready with the flashlight.

Tilda lay quiet and waited for her father to settle into his reading. Stacked books filled the parlor. During the day, they raided libraries, seeking the old tomes of the old world, those that weren't yet moldy and pulped. Father taught her how to read for the day when the shadows went home. He promised that day would come, and the people could be free again.

She adjusted the dial on the oil lamp, amplifying the single flame then climbed out of bed. The floor chilled her bare feet, and Tilda moved to the window. She pushed over a rocking chair, pulled herself up to reach the window frame then opened the seal, pulling back the cover a crack, just enough to see into the fields that surrounded their cottage. Steel towers decayed and slowly collapsed beyond the fence, and the dead power lines they carried tangled between the rusting supports. She could just see a line of pine trees at the edge of the field, illuminated by the moonlight. Whenever she missed her mother, she looked to the pregnant moon, round and full once each month.

Tilda searched the grass, scanning for shadow outlines. She spotted no movement but knew it didn't mean anything. They could have been waiting along the walls, hiding in the ever-dark places. Father kept the doors locked and the walls sealed, but sometimes they snuck into the house. Light glowed from the parlor through the crack in her door, and her oil lamp should have been enough to cast them out. She checked her door, watching for father. He'd be furious if he caught her doing this, but Tilda had to know. She unlatched the glass and eased open the window. Frigid air rushed into her bedroom, and she shook in just her nightgown.

"Mom?" she whispered to the Whisperers. The wind murmured. She could hear them just on the edge. They were coming, summoned by the new shadows she'd cast off like bait. The shadow people swooped in like crows for the little carrion in the grass. "Mom. Are you there?"

". . . here . . ." she whispered, though Tilda couldn't really tell if the being spoke with a feminine inflection. The voice scratched her ears.

"Where are you?" Tilda asked. She wanted to see her mother, to be comforted in her bed and sung to. Somehow in the dark world, her mother always made her feel safer, even with monsters clawing at the windows. Then, she got sad. It rained inside her soul, and she drowned in the flood.

"So close," she whispered.

"Why did you get so sad?" Tilda asked. Tilda still remembered that night when Father fell asleep earlier, the day after she'd taken Tilda into the old city to see the place where she grew up. Mother had been so lost, and she left the cottage, shut the door behind her and walked into the night without a sound.

"I'm not sad. I'm so so happy. I'm dancing in the grass with bare feet. It feels so cool, and I'm so alive. You should leave that place, crawl out your window and dance with me."

"You . . . won't hurt me?"

"Of course not," the voice said. "You are my daisy chain." The voice whispered closer. She could feel its pressure tickling along her neck. Tilda's heart beat faster.

"Why can't you come home?" Tilda asked.

"I am home. I am free, and you could be too. We could be together." How could her mother ever want to hurt her? She had come home, and maybe it would be alright to dance in the grass for a while under the moonlight. "I never meant to leave you," the voice whispered. Tilda stood up on the rocking chair handle, balancing herself to pull through the window. She'd just fit. Black tentacles oozed along the walls and frame. Black mouth opened and reached for the girl. As she climbed, Tilda slammed the chair against the wall. A moment later, Father ran into the bedroom.

"Don't listen to it!" he yelled. Father carried a flashlight and dragged a cable behind him. He kept the light plugged into a car battery, saving it for invasions, and he burned the wall, window and Tilda in blinding light. The shadow screeched and yanked back its tentacles from the house.

"Father. You don't understand. It was Mom. She wasn't going to hurt me. She's just . . . different."

"They eat up all the little girls," he said, whipping the window and the outside grounds with the light. Several shadows fled the grass, cutting humanoid patterns into the moonlight. He slammed the window, sealed the shutters then picked up Tilda by her arms. "She whispers to me at night," he said. "I read to block her voice out." He set Tilda down on the bed then pulled over the rocking chair.

"Why did she leave us?"

His voice calmed. "I don't know, baby." Tilda got under the covers. Father burned the walls, checking every corner, each shadow cast by the bed or dresser, checking under the collage he'd made for his daughter out of dried daisies. She knew he worried one of the shadow people had gotten in and was hiding, waiting for him to let his guard down. After searching for several minutes, he sat on the rocking chair and watched his daughter, waiting for her to sleep. Father yawned several times, and finally, he extinguished the flashlight, needing to save the battery. He kept it ready. The wind picked up and blew against the wall of the house, reminding the mortals within of its power.

"It's not your mother," he said. "My Mary is lost."

"I heard her," Tilda said. She wept into her arm, hiding her eyes. "She wanted me to dance with her. She called me her —"

"You were too young to remember when they came," he said. "In one night, they devoured the world. A single shadow could eat a town. Your mother is dead. Now, sleep."

Tilda shut her eyes. She'd have the daylight tomorrow while he slept. Maybe she could find her mother and talk to her from a safe distance. Mother always liked the city. Father had forbidden Tilda to go, but she could slip by him when he finally collapsed from exhaustion. He just didn't understand.

❧

In the morning, Father slept. Tilda dressed, ignoring his warnings from the night before. It was the daytime, and she could hide among the light, keep it cloaked to her body and keep the shadows away. Her mother lived in the shadows. She'd never really hurt Tilda. How could she?

Tilda dressed and packed some bread to take with her. She'd follow the overgrown roads into the city. The earth took back Philadelphia. Blueberry bushes infested the old buildings and bridges. Weeds picked at the roads. Mom had shown her once just after dawn, told her of the old world. Father slept by her bed. He'd sleep for the next few hours, and Tilda could slip in and out without disturbing him. He'd never know Tilda had left.

She left their cottage and cut through the tall grass. Tilda watched the shadows like she had been taught. The shadows could live in the grass, among the tall blades and snatch you as you walked by the darkness. She followed the cracked road to the city, stepping over the weeds that pulverized the concrete and tar. Train tracks ran at a distance. The road scaled bridges, and apartment buildings decayed around her. Rusting cars dripped oil. The old world decayed around. She passed an overturned train, the same train her mother had pointed out when they first walked this path. *I used to take that train.* Her mother had told her. Your grandmother lived in these buildings. *They swept her away. I miss her. I miss my mother.*

She had faint memories of her mother's old apartment building, but she followed the road, stepping through the alleys between the decayed structures. Creeper plants and bushes grew up into the walls, perching in the cracks between the brick. A city bus rusted in the middle of the avenue. Its windows had shattered, and it looked as if the passengers and driver had been collected while making a routine stop.

Was this the building? She remembered the awnings decayed with green patina. Her mother had pointed out that hydrant. As children, they played in the water, cooling in the hot water. Her mother's face had drawn so pale when she spoke of the happy past, exposing a sadness that her daughter even at such a young age recognized. Tilda picked up a concrete piece and tossed it a pile of collapsed wood and drywall that had dumped from the first level of the building. A board fell, altering the path of the shadows cast from the pile. The Whisperers slithered and curled, adjusting to the change in their dens. Tilda stood back.

"The eye of heaven never stops burning," a man said. He stumbled down the broken avenue. "Tried eating stone, but it shattered my teeth. Want to see?" The bald and burned fellow exposed his jaw and showed a mouth full of chipped teeth. She backed away. The only thing more dangerous than the Whisperers were the people left in the world.

"I don't have any food," she said. She could handle the shadows—just stay out of the dark—but she hadn't expected to encounter anyone in the lost city. They survived by living in the open, away from anything that blocked the free sun.

"Of course you do, my little morsel." Tomato flesh covered him—cracked and dried from constant sun. The sunburn devoured his skin, eating up his body. Body sores ripped tears down his face and arms, showing bone and muscle. A breeze blew past his rancid body, and she gagged, fighting back vomit. "Lots to eat," tomato-man said. "We all got to eat. Only a few of us left. They'll be gone soon now. I know why the shadows leaked."

"Why did they come?"

"They whisper from the corners and tell me their ways. They sweep from world to world, gorging themselves and nourishing their kind. A part of the natural systems of the universe. The wheels turn. A species gets too big, and they come to thin the ranks. Their hunger will be sated soon. Oh yes. But not mine."

"Stay back," she said, searching the ground for another concrete hunk. She couldn't lift the ones she found. He lurched forward, stumbling on untied and rotting shoe leather and grabbed a board from the rubbish pile in front of the building. The pile collapsed, dropping stone and wood and steel poles. It shifted the shadows and crossed the dark with his. The serpent wrapped tight around his leg and slithered up his body. He yanked at the fetter but couldn't rip free. It fed under his tattered trousers and soaked through his burnt skin. The tomato-man's body imploded. His soiled clothing dropped to the road.

Tilda ran until her bones ached and didn't look back at the city. She ran so fast, she didn't always see the shadows. Twice, she stepped into the midnight puddles and felt the bottom of her shoe grabbed. She had to surrender one to break free. Father would be awake soon.

☙

Father searched the grass for her, weeping into the fields. He cut back the blades with a scythe, but it would have taken a year to clear the plains that grew up around the cottage. Tilda hadn't meant to be so late. The sun already set. She could tell from Father's vacant eyes, he thought she had been taken and consumed by the shadows. Father looked up and saw her, then he ran to Tilda.

"You're still here!"

"I'm so sorry, Father. I needed to find Mom."

He grabbed her by the arm and yanked her into the house. "You went into the old city looking for her. You killed me, Matilda."

"I just needed to see her, and if I couldn't find her, I needed to see where she lived."

"That world is dead! It'll never come back. Stop looking to the past."

He sat her at the kitchen table and boiled her some spinach. The soup tasted bland and the fronds were few. The garden had not grown the food they needed for the winter, and the game ran fewer. They spoke little into the evening as the darkness drew over the cottage and over the world. Finally, she volunteered what she had learned:

"It won't be forever," she said.

"What do you mean?" Father searched the walls, checking for cracks and gaps in the defenses of the walls.

"A man tried to eat me today," she said. "I didn't mean for it to happen."

"See what happens when you go into the city?" Father asked.

"I miss her," she said. Tears dripped into her soup.

"I miss her too. But I have to go on. For you. For the species."

His face never recovered from the ashen color. He'd thought he'd lost his daughter, and his life sank into the mud below the grass. When night fell, Father didn't make Tilda go to bed. They sat on the old couch, curled up around the cast iron stove he had salvaged, and grasped at the sparse warmth.

The voice whispered but spoke loud enough to be heard by father and daughter: "Let me in, my family."

"You are dead," Father said to the door.

"No. I exist. The dark ones teach us so much. They tell us how to truly be. I want my family to be with me."

Father wrapped a wool blanket around Tilda's shoulders to keep her warm. "Don't listen," he said, but she could see his face changing. He waivered. Father felt as she did, falling into the trap. Tilda would always remember this night, and I wondered if it was her fault.

"Will you take us to the stars?"

"I will, my family." Father sighed and fed another twig into the cast-iron stove. The warmth barely registered in the house, and she shivered under the blanket. Mom's word pricked Tilda's skin, and she tightened the blanket around her shoulders. "Open the door. Let me ride the shadows to your world."

"I can't. Our daughter."

"It's not Mom, right?"

"I don't know," Father said.

"Open the door," Tilda pleaded. "Please open the door. They will be gone soon and Mom will go with them."

Father hesitated at the portal, and his lip quivered. His knuckles bleached white when he gripped the handle.

"It'll be like it was," the Whisperer whispered. "Our family together." Father sighed, unlocked the door then allowed the shadow to enter the house. Tilda stood behind him, trembling, waiting to be touched, consumed and taken to wherever Mom waited. A shadow silhouette danced at the door with elegant limb. She swirled and twirled and reached for father, wrapping her tendrils around his chest. Father sucked in a breath, and the ink poured down his nose and mouth, filling his body. His robes fell and spilled onto the wooden floor of the cabin. Tilda closed her eyes and waited. She reached for her father and knelt on the floor by his robes. There, she fell into sleep, waiting.

The rising sun cast its orange light through the doorway, waking the girl.

"Mom, don't go without me! Please!"

ભ

T. Fox Dunham *resides outside of Philadelphia PA – author and historian. He's published in nearly 200 international journals and anthologies. His first novel,* The Street Martyr *was published by Gutter Books this October, followed* Professional Detachment, *a literary erotica from Bitten Press and followed by* Searching for Andy Kaufman *from PMMP in 2014. He's a cancer survivor. His friends call him fox, being his totem animal, and his motto is: Wrecking civilization one story at a time.*

Site: www.tfoxdunham.com.
Blog: http://tfoxdunham.blogspot.com/. http://www.facebook.com/tfoxdunham
& Twitter: @TFoxDunham

NO EVE

RICHARD FARREN BARBER

The last woman on earth stood in the hallway. There was a knock on the front door.

Darkness crowded around Christine. The candle she held guttered in the draft and for a moment the yellow flame painted a huge Christine-esque shadow on the far wall. The image looked like it might lean over and devour her. Christine looked away. There was no need for her imagination to produce false monsters when the world was full of real ones.

She held the candle out in front of her, but the amount of light it produced was pitiful. It picked out some of the photographs along the walls and she could see the carpet under her feet, but she could not see the door until she was next to it.

The piece of wood that she had nailed across the door frame held fast when she tested it. Her old woodwork teacher would be appalled if he saw the crooked nails and rough wood, but at least it had worked so far. The hammer she had used lay on the floor, the silver head reflecting the candle's flame.

The knocking on the door started again.

"Go away," she shouted.

The knock on the door stopped. The silence that followed seemed thicker than Christine remembered. It was as if the air in the hallway was filled with cotton wool. Had he gone? Could it really be that easy? She leant inward and tried to pick up the sound of the man's breathing. Because she was certain that he was still out there.

Oh, a sly one this time, she thought. *Trying to lure me out.* Maybe he had learned from all the others.

"It won't work," she called out to him. Her words flattened against the walls and she imagined that they would not reach through the door. The man would be sitting on the step unaware that Christine had ever spoken.

She sat down, feeling the carpet brush the bare backs of her legs. Her spine pressed against the door and her head touched the wood just below the letterbox. There was a thick plank of wood covering the slot in the door, with large silver nails sticking out at angles. It wasn't pretty, but then it hadn't needed to be. She wasn't auditioning for a part in *Home Makeovers* or *DIY Queens*. The slab of wood across the letterbox was functional.

She twisted round and stared at the door. The recessed panels were worn, the grain showing through. James had promised to paint it someday, but it seemed that the end of the world had made a liar of her husband.

"I'm not going to let you in," she told him. "It doesn't matter what you say."

He was silent and Christine had to stop herself from saying anything else. Maybe that was what he wanted, maybe that was his plan. It seemed to her that these days everyone had a plan. Everyone had a strategy.

Everyone except her. The closest she had to a plan was her determination to keep out the horde.

She opened her mouth to tell him. He'd be much better getting up from her doorstep and running to stay as far from the horde as possible, but she closed her mouth without speaking. To have survived out there he already knew more about the horde then she could tell him. Instead she stood up, trying to avoid making any noise, and she walked to the far end of the hallway. She held the hammer in her right hand, the candle in her left.

She walked into the kitchen, easing the door closed behind her, but the snick of the catch sounded like a gunshot.

The kitchen was too large. Before, it had seemed just right, but now the light from the candle didn't reach into the corners of the room. Christine had learned that when she couldn't see the walls of the room her imagination would fill in the gaps.

She hurried across to the back door and began to check the bolts and the planks of wood that fastened the door to the frame. Once she was done she climbed onto the chair by the sink. When she placed her hand on the wood panel she could hear the crunch of broken glass. She checked the panels and decided that for now at least they would suffice, she didn't fancy hammering more nails into the wood while someone was hanging around the place.

She jumped down and opened the door to the hallway. He was still there, she could feel him. She tiptoed across the hallway, and when she reached the safety of the bottom step she paused for a moment. As she ascended the staircase she kept to the edge, where the steps were less likely to creak beneath her weight.

Her patrol of the upstairs rooms was undertaken with the same thoroughness she had given to the lower rooms. She knew it was almost impossible that they would be able to force an entry up here, but Christine was sure her belt-and-braces approach to security had kept her alive this long. She checked the shutters over the windows and the locks on the inside of the doors. Everything remained solid. She tried not to consider the circumstance under which she would need to take refuge in one of the upstairs rooms.

In one of the lengths of wood covering the building at the front of the house there was a knothole. She had left it there deliberately to provide a small viewpoint over the surrounding land. There were times when she would come up to this room and stare out at the empty fields surrounding the house, just to remind herself of a world which was not all dark shadows and the smell of burning candles.

Christine looked out. The horizon was empty. The land around used to be golden with wheat, but the crops had been destroyed and all that remained was the brown earth leaching to a uniform dust-grey. It was impossible for Christine to imagine a time when the crops might grow again, when the world might return to anything approaching normal. These were the end days that the preacher had crowed about on the only radio station that was still broadcasting. She had listened for a few minutes, but the man's voice had infected her with his harsh phrases about the wrath of God and the fall of woman.

The knothole did not allow her to look down to the front step of her house. Before that had never been an issue, but now Christine found herself wishing that she had done something about that flaw while she could. She stood on tiptoes and tried to squint down, but she could only see the gate at the front of the house. It was shut. He had shut it after him.

Christine wasn't sure whether that was comforting or disturbing. She stepped back from the knothole and allowed the thin shaft of sunlight to pierce through the hole and hit the floor of the room once more.

She went back downstairs and crept up to the front door. She put the flat of her palm on the wood, as if she might feel the man on the other side.

"You might as well go," she said quietly.

"Why?" he whispered back. Her immediate response was an urgent need to check all the boards and locks and shutters around the house again, to make absolutely certain that the horde could not find any way inside. The temptation was almost impossible to resist.

She clenched her hands into tight fists that she held against the sides of her hips. *No,* she said to herself, *I won't let him frighten me like that.*

But the horde... the horde was coming.

Christine shook her head to get rid of the Radio Preacher. It seemed that now, when her mind needed to deliver any bad thoughts to her, it always chose the same voice.

"You can't come in," she told him.

"Absolutely not!" The man on the other side of the door sounded appalled at the suggestion. "You can't allow anyone inside."

Christine sat down on the floor, her back against the wall. "You understand," she whispered.

"I can see you've had your troubles."

"What..." Christine struggled to ask the question, realising that maybe ignorance was better. "What...can you see?"

The man's voice was sad and kind, and as he spoke Christine imagined herself sitting opposite him on a train. They would talk for a while and part as friends. Nothing life-changing, just the shared comfort of a few hours together.

"There is...blood," he said, and Christine found the way he hesitated before saying the word endearing, as if he thought he could protect her. "Not as much as I would have expected. But you have been visited."

"Yes."

"It must have been terrible."

Christine closed her eyes. She heard the echoes of the screams as they leaked from the walls. She heard the clash of metal blades and then the duller sound of weapons upon flesh. She had cried then, and she found herself crying now. Soft, soundless weeping. Amongst the voices was the sound of James's screaming. She put her hands over her ears but it did no good because it was an echo from weeks before.

She wasn't sure how much she missed of what the man on the other side of the door said. His voice slipped in through the grief. Tentative. Cool.

"I am just resting here. I will go soon."

"Please do," Christine said. "They will be back. I know they will." There was silence, but she imagined the man on the other side of the door nodding his head in sage-like wisdom. Of course they would be back.

In her mind he had a large, black, bushy beard, blue eyes and a thinning mop of curly black hair. He would be thin and tired, because these days everyone who was still alive was thin and tired. Christine had heard enough from the men and boys who came knocking at her door pleading for sanctuary and declaring how hungry they were and promising that they were no part of the horde. This man was different. This man had asked for nothing.

"How have you survived?" Christine asked. "You must have come across the horde."

"I keep moving and I have been lucky. So far I have only seen the horde from a distance."

She tried to imagine him out on the road. In her mind she saw the man with his black beard, sleeping fitfully beneath a tree and rising before the horde approached.

"Don't you feel them?" Christine asked. "Don't you feel their hunger?" She had found herself returning to the question in her dark moments, and now she had the opportunity to ask it.

"You have a good site here," he told her. "I can see down the valley. Nothing can surprise you."

She didn't comment on her unanswered question, but her cheeks burned. "Where will you go from here?" Christine asked.

"South."

She waited for him to say more, but he offered nothing else. Just south.

"What's your name?"

The silence lasted so long that Christine started to think that the man had not heard her. She was considering repeating her question when he finally replied.

"It's better that you don't know."

"Why?"

"I will be gone from here soon. It will be easier for you if I am just a voice. That way you won't feel guilty."

"I'm not guilty."

"I know," the man said. "You're not guilty and neither am I and neither is anyone who has joined the horde."

Christine tried to decide if he was trying to make her open the door. Nothing in his voice suggested this; he sounded like he genuinely did not want her to know any more about him than she already did. She wanted to shout at him: *Just go then, if that's what you think!* But she was afraid that if she did then he would take her advice and she would be alone once more. Even if he was on the other side of the door from her, even if this was just a temporary arrangement before he continued on his way, there was comfort to be had from this closeness, from contact with another person.

The candle flame began to flicker as it consumed the wick. Christine watched the yellow light and realised that soon the flame would die. Maybe that would not be so bad. Maybe to spend her last days in perfect darkness would be better.

She rose to her feet.

"What's wrong?" the man asked.

"My candle has almost burned out."

"You have light?" the man said. The awe in his voice was impossible to conceal. "You have a flame?"

"Candles," Christine said. "I have to be careful because my supply will run out soon."

"You were well prepared for this disaster."

"James," she said. "Not me, it was James."

She hurried away from the door before the man could ask her any further questions. Her cheeks were damp and she sniffed to draw the tears away from her eyes.

She battered open the door into the kitchen and the sound crashed through the building. Now she was not concerned about making too much noise. Now she did not tiptoe through the dark house but instead smashed and banged her way into the room. She was sick of feeling like she was living in a tomb, waiting for the horde to descend upon her once more and this time tear the house apart until it was able to get at her. She was sick of pushing away every memory of James, as if remembering him made her weaker.

She dragged the back of her hand across her eyes.

The candles were in a box at the back of the cupboard, where James had left them. The one she held was a small nub of hot wax and she pulled out a new, white stem. Although it was cowardice, she made a point of not looking into the box to see how many candles were left.

When she returned, the man called, "Where did you go?" but she chose not to answer him. She could keep secrets too.

"My name is Christine," she told him. Part of her mind was screaming that it was a terrible mistake to tell him this, that she needed him to be gone. Life was hard enough; she didn't need to complicate it any further.

"Nice to meet you, Christine," the man said. He didn't offer his own name.

"They'll come again," Christine said. As soon as she spoke she realised how terrified she was of the prospect. The memory of the hard voices of the horde battering the sides of her house seemed like a nightmare to her now. The candle wavered in her hand and she put it on the floor so that the light shone steadfast and constant: her corner of the hallway bathed in a comforting yellow glow. She picked up the hammer. The weight in her hand offered her more comfort than the light.

"James said..." she started to tell the man, but she was appalled at the confidence she had nearly betrayed and she shut her mouth fast.

"I know," the man said, so softly he might have been sitting beside her. "I've been there too. You have to forget what happened at the end and just remember him as he was. Can you do that?"

"Yes," Christine said automatically, but on her side of the door she shook her head in denial because every memory of her husband was tainted. The horde had arrived at the house and James had stood on the porch. As she hammered home the nails to secure first the front door and then the back door and then the letterbox James had urged her to, "Hurry, hurry."

The horde crashed down upon the house like a storm. For a moment she heard James fighting against them, but then his voice was subsumed within the horde and shortly afterwards he was one of them — his curses and shouts all the more terrible because she recognised his voice.

"What happened in the end — that wasn't him."

"Do you...Did you have a wife?" Christine asked, blundering into the question in her haste to turn the conversation away from James.

"No," the man said, but Christine sensed a layer of complexity beneath such a simple answer. From his voice she put him in his thirties, and maybe he didn't have a wife, or a girlfriend, but there was someone there.

"She died," he said. "At the time it was terrible. At the time I thought it was the worst thing that could ever happen to me. But now, because of this, I think that maybe it was for the best. At least I don't have to worry about her or think about what the horde would do to her. What I would do to her."

"What was her name?"

"No. I won't tell you. I have to go."

The door shuddered in its frame and Christine imagined the man leaning against it as he pulled himself to his feet.

"Please don't go, not yet."

"They will be here soon. I need to get away."

"Not yet."

"I can feel them, Christine."

Terror washed through her. For a moment she was blind. Christine stood up and put the palms of her hands flat against the door to steady herself.

"What do you mean?"

"I can feel them. I have done for a while now. While we've been sitting here talking I've been arguing with myself about how long I can stay before it's too late. Before I'm dangerous."

She didn't know if it was just because of what he said, but now Christine thought she could detect something else in the man's voice—a degree of strain that had not been there when she had started speaking to him. Her first reaction was to tell him to leave, to get as far away from her as possible. Had she said the same thing to James?

"They will be here soon."

She stepped away from the door, knocking the candle with the heel of her shoe so that it splashed light across the walls. She bent down to pick it up and hurried away, her feet echoing through the empty house. She rushed up the stairs and into the front bedroom where the slice of sunlight cut through the darkness. She put her eye to the knothole and looked out onto the valley.

The valley was empty. Nothing moved. No animals. No trees. No clouds. It was as if the world had been set on pause. She imagined the thin track that wound along the bottom of the valley filled with men, like a river of hate.

"There's no-one out there," she called down to the man, even though she knew that he would not be able to hear her.

And then she saw the movement at the cleft where the two mountains dipped to join each other. It was too far away for her to see any details of the horde, and too far for her to hear anything, but she watched their steady approach.

She ran downstairs, her feet thumping on bare wooden risers.

"They're here," she said. The words scratched at her throat.

She could sense his fear even through the locked door. Anger blossomed in her chest. *What do you have to be frightened of?* She thought. *They're here for me, not you.* She batted the harsh thought away: James had been frightened in the end.

"I have a gun," the man said.

The statement confused Christine. She couldn't decide if it was a threat. Was he trying to force himself inside?

The house was empty of weapons. She had taken an inventory while James had stood on the porch. She had nothing with which to protect herself except for the hammer.

"You need to leave," Christine said, trying to keep her voice neutral. "They will be here soon."

She thought of James standing on the porch. Not James as he looked on that last day, but instead her mind played a trick on her and she remembered her husband as a much younger man, a man only just out of University, before his hair had faded from black to grey. He had a beard then, that first year she had met him.

She waited in silence. She could feel the man on the other side of the door and occasionally she heard the creak of a wooden board when he shifted his weight. He said nothing and she imagined the view from where he stood as he watched the horde filling up the valley. What would it be now—a thousand men strong? Maybe more? She found it impossible to imagine a number larger than a thousand.

There was a long silence until she heard the crunch of boots and shoes and trainers on the gravel lane. She heard the rumble of their voices. She smelled them—their stench pervaded the house, as if taking possession of it. Taking possession of her.

Panic flooded her and she started to attack the bolts with her hands, tearing at the metal.

"What are you doing?" he called.

"You need to come inside, Jim," she called.

"No."

The bolt at the top of the door was stiff and she needed both hands to pull it free from its housing. It made a loud sound in the stillness of the empty corridor, like a prison cell slamming shut.

"No," he said again. She heard the shock in his voice. "They're nearly at your gate. Don't you understand?"

The second bolt opened with ease and then the door was only held closed by the layers of old boards that she had hammered across the frame. She took up the hammer and started clawing at the nails that she dimly remembered smashing into place in a frenzy. The first nail bent when she tried to pry it loose and instead she swung the head of the hammer at the door, achieving nothing but a round dent in the wooden board.

She heard the man's voice rise to a shout as he tried to reason with the horde. He told them to turn away. He told them that they were better than this. He told them that the house was empty.

And the horde jeered at him with a hungry voice and accused him of wanting to keep the woman for himself.

Christine reached up and pushed home the bolt. She did so quietly, hoping the man outside would not hear her betrayal.

She had never heard a gunshot before, not close up. It sounded like a cannon firing and the reverberations ran through her chest. She smelled the cordite seeping in through tiny cracks in the door.

In the silence that followed she wondered if the man had taken his own life. She wondered if he was lying on her front porch, blood seeping from a huge hole in the side of his head where the bullet had wrecked a trail through his brains.

Coward, she thought, and immediately she felt guilty — aware that there was no reason why she should hold the monopoly on terror.

The gun fired again. There was something terrible about the silence after each shot, and she wanted to shout to the man — ask him what he was doing or what had happened. Not knowing was its own form of torture. But she couldn't shout because there was the horde to consider — the throng of men armed with axes and crowbars and anything else that could be used as a weapon. The horde which had ravaged through the country. Husbands turning on their wives. Fathers on their daughters. Sons on their mothers. The horde which was now a living thing which devoured all the women of the land, seeking them out, until there was only Christine left. She was sure of it. She was sure that she was the last woman in the world.

The gun fired a third time. Through the thick door she heard the voice of the horde. Although there were no words she heard the hatred which burned within them. She wondered what would become of them once she was gone. Once there were no more women, then they would no longer have a purpose. Would the horde just dissolve? Melt away into the constituent individuals who might still remember what they had done whilst they were caught up inside the fever?

Is that what happened to James?

There was a loud bang on the door which caused the whole structure to shudder, and immediately Christine assumed the man was dead. The horde had reached the house.

"Help me," the man said.

He was still alive? It wasn't possible.

He banged his fist upon the door again. "Let me in," he shouted at her. "For God's sake, please let me in. There are too many of them."

She wanted to run away from his voice, to hide in the farthest corner of the house so she didn't have to listen to the terror that drenched every word he spoke. His fists beat against the door. She tried to tell herself that it was too late to do anything to save him, even though she knew that she was lying to herself. She kept the door closed because she had to. Because that was the only way to survive.

But she wouldn't run. She owed him at least that much respect.

The man's gun fired for a fourth time, but it sounded muffled and Christine wondered whether this was because the horde was now too close. She imagined him standing on the porch, almost exactly where James had stood just a few weeks earlier.

The front door shuddered under the impact of the horde's arrival. If possible, the sound was even louder than the gunshot had been. She heard the timbers of the porch creaking under the weight of the mass of bodies. Something hit the door: an axe, maybe. Not enough to penetrate through the wood, but Christine knew that this would be next.

From along the corridor came a rattling which suggested that the back of the house were also being tested. The chime of falling glass betrayed their progress. They had reached the large window over the sink. She hoped that they cut their hands to ribbons on the broken glass. But there would be others, that was the truth of the horde; there were always others.

The blade of an axe punched through a panel on the front door and a sliver of light pierced the dark hallway. It speared through the gloom and struck the carpet near the staircase. Now that the wood was punctured Christine knew that it would not be much longer before the door was broken entirely.

She backed away from the front door, until she stood at the foot of the stairs. The candle flame jumped in her hand and the shadows cast upon the walls were huge animals that pounced in the light.

If anything, the back of the house was even more exposed. A patchwork of timber planks crossed over the gap where the large window had been, and from where she stood in the hallway Christine heard the tortured sound of the wood been prised apart. Within seconds the gloom of the kitchen had been ripped asunder and the room was filled with sunlight that washed out of the door and along the corridor. When it touched Christine she felt like she had been burned.

She watched hands tearing at the wooden barricade. Gnarled fingers reached between the planks and pulled at the nails, easing them out. Blood ran down their wrists, but she knew that they felt nothing of the pain from their ripped fingers.

She could scream, but what use would that do?

Christine ran up the stairs and into the front bedroom. She looked out through the knothole onto a valley drowning in men. They surrounded the house, too many to count. They stood in disorganised rows and each of them held some sort of weapon. Most stood and looked up at the window, as if they knew exactly where she was hiding. She felt their hunger breaking against her house. Their hunger for her.

The men mostly stood and watched, their bodies swaying back and forth like a plantation of new saplings caught in a breeze. Flashes of sunlight caught the edges of blades. Occasionally there would be movement as one man pushed between the others to reach the front.

And yet below her she knew that the horde was still burrowing through her fragile defences. She could hear the scratch of hands upon wood as they prised away her makeshift protection.

She started to pull away the wooden barrier from the window, tearing at the planks with her fingers. One plank came free from the others and revealed a slice of the outside world. She started work on a second, aware that in the background the low murmur of the horde was growing louder. She would not die in the dark, she promised herself.

She heard their footsteps in the hallway downstairs, and then the clatter of their feet on the staircase as they rose to meet her.

She locked the door, and cast around her for something to prop it closed, but the room was empty of anything useful. She held the hammer clenched tightly in her two hands, ready to bring it down through the skull of the first man who entered the room.

The last woman on earth stood in the light of a summer day. There was a bang on the door.

☙

Richard Farren Barber *was born in Nottingham in July 1970. After studying in London he returned to the East Midlands. He lives with his wife and son and works as an Operations Manager for a local university.*

He has written over 200 short stories and has had short stories published in Alt-Dead, Alt-Zombie, Blood Oranges, Derby Scribes Anthology, Derby Telegraph, ePocalypse – Tales from the End, Horror D'Oeuvres, Murky Depths, Midnight Echo, Midnight Street, Morpheus Tales, MT Biopunk Special, MT Urban Horror Special, Night Terrors II, Siblings, The House of Horror, Trembles, When Red Snow Melts, *and broadcast on* BBC Radio Derby *and* The Wicked Library.

Richard's novella, "The Power of Nothing" was published by Damnation Books in September 2013 and his next novella, "The Sleeping Dead" will be published in August 2014 by DarkFuse.

His website can be found here www.richardfarrenbarber.co.uk

AMBER SKYLIGHTS

FRANCISCO J. IBANEZ

The crashing, frantic footsteps got closer and closer until they stopped. Sarah did her best to control her breathing, but she could swear the men would be able to hear the blood rushing through her veins like an overflowing, angry river.

"We know you're out here," the gruff voice ripped through the darkness like a saw. "We ain't gonna hurt ya, lady. We just wanna know where ya get your water. That's it. Hand to God." One of the men retched and spit.

Yeah, right, she thought to herself.

Judging by the sound of their clumsy footfalls she was sure there were only two of them. The men split up and began searching for her with the grace of tumbling cinderblocks. After waiting a few minutes, she crept out from behind the sheet metal hiding spot, stood up, and braced herself against the edge of a half broken and burned concrete wall. She peered around the side and saw one of them approaching her position. This one was ragged and dirty. His lanky frame did little to fill out his ill-fitting clothes. He looked exhausted. His breathing seemed abnormal. The other man was nowhere to be seen or heard.

She reared her knife-wielding left arm across her chest and formed the beginnings of a fist with her right hand. With her face pressed sideways against the wall, she waited until she saw the beginning of his grimy profile.

His breathing became louder and his thin, scrawny face broke her field of vision. He was almost a foot taller than her. She did a half-spin towards him and her small, granite fist smashed into his nose with a vicious and accurate crunch. The man's eyes teared and slammed shut, and his hands instinctively clawed at his broken face. Blood poured out between his fingers. Taking advantage of his blindness, she reared back and crashed her fist into his loose stomach. He fell to his knees and bent over moaning with the back of his dirty neck exposed. She raised her left arm with the knife pointing downward and brought the barbaric point of her blade down into his neck, plunged it to the guard, and through the front of his throat. His spinal cord was sliced in two. The man dropped to his face. The sound of his final exhalation gurgling through his torn windpipe was his last will and testament to the blood soaked ground.

Her veins felt as if they were carrying lightning instead of blood. She looked around. The other man was nowhere in sight. She wanted to search the dead one but decided it was better to make a quick escape.

She had gotten fifty yards away when she heard coarse screaming, "Goddamn you! I'm going to catch you, you little bitch! Just wait, you can't hide forever!"

Thanks for letting me know where you are, she thought. Sarah crawled alongside a long line of abandoned and charred vehicles that littered a useless main street. Taking the long way home and being extra cautious took an extra three hours, but it was worth it. She still had her secret water-traps, but more importantly she still had her life. She remained in her home for a week straight, and when she finally came out her every move was careful and precise. She did not want to deal with the remaining man anytime soon.

೮೩

It was easy to walk outside and forget you still lived on earth. The smells of flora and fauna had been replaced by the smells of a dying and corroding world. Smoldering pieces of plastic, fantastic fires half put out, creatures and objects of all sorts slowly being reverted back to their most basic of biological elements. Everything eaten away as much by fire and acid-rain as by the pillaging and salvaging that occurred daily. The noises carried by the winds were unnatural, sometimes caused by decrepit buildings slowly swaying back and forth until finally giving up and diving to the rust and charcoal-stained ground, as if by choice.

The smog-filtered sunshine forced Sarah to perceive her world as if looking through the bottoms of amber-colored beer bottles. She lived alone in her hand-formed hut that mimicked a pile of dried mud and trash. It was inconspicuous, safe, and sturdy. It was easier this way, and honestly, anything that was easy was to be taken advantage of without a moment's notice. The rules had mutated. Those that stuck by the old rules did not last long.

☙

It was dark when Sarah stepped out of her home, inhaled a breath that smelled and tasted like a dumpster fire, and looked out into the sky. It was clear and still. The violence that stuck to everything like rusty fish-scales was cloaked by the drowning of the sun. She saw a crushed, grey pop-can lying on its side. It reminded her of Micah. The thought dragged her into sadness....

☙

Three years ago, she had been out hunting when she noticed a couple of people building something to live in using junk and debris. She spied on them for a few weeks. They were strangers; a threat until proven otherwise. She had to make sure they were not harmful or aggressive. Sarah had noted the man was not well-versed in the art of collecting water, and they were barely surviving on their meager supplies.

The most intriguing aspect of the pair was the young girl that accompanied the older man. She didn't have the drawn out, forlorn expression like everyone else. She wore a look of wonderment that shone through the grit and dirt on her face. After a month, she realized they were not aggressive or threatening, and the girl was most likely the man's daughter. The next day Sarah left a bounty of two liters of water, a cleaned, preserved rat, and a note that read, "The waters clean and the rat is fine to eat."

After three days Sarah returned and waited for the man to leave his home, alone. He did, and she followed him for a mile through the streets of a residential area that had one house as hollow and miserable as a caved in human skull. She snuck up behind him.

"Don't move. I'm not going to hurt you. What's your name?"

She pushed the sharpened end of a homemade spear just below his left shoulder-blade.

The man was startled and he jumped.

"My name is Marc. I'm alone. Take what you want but I beg you to leave me some water."

"I'm not going to rob you, Marc. I just need to know what you're doing here. Just stay relaxed and nothing is going to happen."

"I'm hunting. Or trying, anyways. That's it. What do you want from me?"

"What's your relationship to the girl?"

Sarah noticed Marc's back stiffen and his head come up a fraction of an inch. She knew this was the most dangerous part of the endeavor. There was no telling how the man would now react.

"I don't know what you're talking about. I'm alone here."

"I know there's a girl. I've been watching you two for over a month. I'm not going to hurt you but I need to know if I can trust you. Turn around slowly. I don't want to shove this spear into your heart but I will. Don't test me."

Marc turned around. The rising tension caused the surroundings to take on an even more sinister appearance. The grey clouds in the night sky crawled overhead and the breeze seemed to whisper foreign curses at them. The peeling paint of a nearby burnt house looked like ancient hospital gauze falling away from the old wounds of an exhumed corpse. The pair of survivors stared at each other.

"Okay, good. Nice and easy, Marc. Who's the girl?"

"I am alone."

"I left water and food for you three days ago. I also left a note. I am not here to hurt either of you. I could have harmed both of you by now, if I had wanted. Who is she?"

Marc sighed, resigned. His jacket was patched in places and the zipper was ripped off.

"Her name is Micah. I'm her father. We're not here to hurt anyone. Now what?"

"Okay, good. My name is Sarah. Do you know anyone else in this area? Are more people coming?"

"We don't know anyone else around here. We split off from a larger group. We were ambushed about three months ago. There were fourteen of us. Six adults, six kids, and two old folks. These... bastards...killed our sentry, Adam, and then barged into our camp. They had all sorts of weapons. One of them even had a rifle. They started attacking and slaughtering everyone. And they were laughing. They were enjoying it. One of their women cornered Micah and me. I smashed her face with a brick. That's how we managed to get away. We walked for ten days straight. I have no idea if anyone else survived."

"I'm sorry to hear that. You're not going to survive out here with your water skills. Or lack of, I should say. I can show you how to collect water. In exchange, you help me maintain my water traps and you act like a good neighbor as long as you live in my neighborhood. If you try to trick me or hurt me at any time, I will kill you and I will kill your daughter. Do we understand each other?"

"How do I know you're not tricking me? What insurance do I have that you won't stab me in the back? Micah is all I have left now and I'm not willing to put her in harm's way."

"You don't have any insurance. Like I said, if I had wanted to hurt you you'd both be dead by now. As for the girl, I'm doing this for her. I can help you both. Who knows, maybe you can teach me something, too. Do we have an agreement or not?"

Sarah lowered her spear.

"Okay," said Marc.

ఌ

"Just breathe slowly. Don't think about anything else. Relax. Make a mental note of how strong the wind is and what direction it's blowing from. Adjust your aim if you have to, and inhale. When you've got it locked, exhale and release the rock. You should be dead-on," Sarah instructed the younger girl. Micah picked out a target and raised the loaded slingshot. She took a couple breaths and let go. The rock flew straight but the discolored pop can remained upright.

"Well, at least we don't have to set that one up again," Sarah said, and winked. "It's Okay, we still have a few hours till the sun comes up. Let's keep practicing. You've hit six out of ten and that's pretty good."

"I think I'm starting to get it but I wish I was better. You're right, though, that's one less can we have to fetch," Micah said. "I promise I'll start hitting all of them. Sarah, can I ask you something?"

"Of course, Micah"

"What do you think about letting me tag-along on hunts with you?"

"Little lady, that's not up to me and we both know that."

"Well, yeah, but...I thought maybe you could talk to my dad about that. He trusts you." The younger girl picked up a piece of metal and threw it at nothing. "I don't know. I'd like to help out, too. You know? I could carry your pack..."

Sarah looked at the girl and smiled. She was a quick learner, and quiet. Sarah did not doubt her potential usefulness. Besides, Micah could learn skills while out hunting that she would never learn otherwise.

"I'll discuss it with your father, but what he says goes. Okay?"

"Okay! Thank you!"

"Don't thank me yet. He should be back in about an hour. In the meantime, I want you to go ten for ten this next round. Who knows, you may be aiming at live targets the next time we do this."

Micah's face lit up and her eyes radiated gratitude.

Marc returned with a liter of water.

"Daddy! You're home!"

"Hey, baby! Hi, Sarah." Micah ran into his arms and they hugged. Marc looked at Sarah, "You were right about my water trap. I had the collection tray off-center and on a slant. I bet I was missing and spilling more than half of the water I could've been getting. It's infuriating. But thank you for your advice. It should be fixed now."

"You're getting the hang of it, though. This liter today is more than you brought last week, right? You're moving in the right direction and that's what counts."

"Well, we owe it to you. Thank you."

"Marc, can I talk to you for a minute?" She motioned for him to follow her.

"Sure. What's up?"

They stood a few yards away from Marc's home. Micah pretended not to watch them. There was a steady breeze tonight. It carried a chill that soaked into their bones. Swift-moving clouds in the distance forecasted rain.

"Micah wants to go hunting with me. I told her I had no choice in the matter and it was all up to you. Her marksmanship skills are improving and she really wants to start contributing. That's all I'm going to say."

"Yeah, I was wondering when she'd ask you. She's been getting real antsy lately. I knew it was a matter of time. I don't think I'm ready to let her go out just yet. I trust you, Sarah. Have no doubt about that. I just want wait a little bit longer for this. I don't think she's ready. If you think I'm wrong then let me know."

"Honestly, I think she would learn a lot. I think she would be useful. I would watch her every move and not let anything happen to her. But I understand your position and I respect it."

"Thanks, Sarah. I know it won't be too long before my little girl is out there, hunting and killing. With your help she'll be better than her dad in no time. I won't be able to hold her back much longer."

"Micah's smart, she'll understand. In the meantime we'll just keep practicing."

"I think that's a good idea," Marc smiled. "Looks like rain is headed this way. You could stay and have dinner with us, wait the storm out."

"Thank you, but I ought to be getting back. I can check out a couple traps on the way. I will see you again in about five days."

Sarah shook hands with Marc and turned to yell goodbye at Micah. The younger girl smiled and waved.

CƷ

It was a good night to hunt and it was one of her favorite things to do now. At its core, it was for pure survival. She never let herself forget this. The constant thundering in her belly made her sure of it. It was her way of dealing with the madness and horror that had been heaved onto her lap without any of her consent. When she was feeling humorous, she would pretend that everything she stalked and murdered was a cheating and selfish high-powered human being who had cast a vote in favor of the destruction of her world. She wanted to believe in reincarnation but only if it meant the guilty would come back as something she could stalk, kill, and eat. She wasn't bitter, though. She had learned it was helpful to let her thoughts be themselves, to let them play in the grim and cunning folds of her mind from time to time.

She knew the neighboring terrain, and it's most recent occupants, better than anyone within a three-mile radius. She had taught herself to recognize different landscape features and was keenly aware of when they changed. Different disasters occurred and erased her landmarks. Chemical fires would start up with no warning and devour huge piles of trash and rubble in an angry symphony of popping and crackling noises, their flames different colors depending on the fuel source. After gorging themselves into non-existence the evidence of their hunger was like that of a crematory oven after being used. Unfortunately, their smells could sometimes be unceremoniously similar. She had been terrible witness to the demise of other living creatures in this way.

It had been raining when Sarah decided to visit the Willems and collect water from their traps along the way. The droplets changed color as they struck the charcoal ground. After walking for two and a half hours, she detected the scent of a trash fire mixed with burning flesh. She ran through ankle-deep sludge and came upon a hellish golden-glow just over the rise. She continued on and ended up staring at the hissing inferno of the trash heap that had been the secret home of Marc Willem and his twelve year old daughter. Sarah had smelled their death throes before she had consciously recognized their demise. There was nothing she could have done. She stifled tears and did her best not to run at the fire and kick and punch it with all her might. She wanted to yell at the sky and tear at the Earth. She did nothing. Despite being raised in a hopeless, despair-ridden existence, Micah, the young girl, had been a vibrant and curious blue-eyed beauty. She had loved and emulated Sarah.

Sarah did not collect water that night. She sat covered and waited seven hours for the fire to burn out. When she finally stood, the sun had started its patterned journey west. Her nails had dug furrows into her palms. A pile of ashes the size of a big car was all there was left. Sarah sighed. She turned around and headed back towards her home. Her eyes were hardly able to contain the unbridled rage and misery that flooded her thoughts.

◌

The cloudless night permitted effortless star ward tracking and easier hunting. Always alert, she spotted something fifteen yards out and stopped her forward movement, her sinewy physique in a state of relaxed tension. Her sharp eyes maintained their vigil and the loaded slingshot was raised as the thick rubber-bands were drawn back to her cheek. She waited. Only a few loose strands of her auburn hair stirred. The glint that had caught her initial attention returned, and the slingshot's ammo was launched through the air. The rat's death was noiseless. That made a total of four so far.

Stopping only long enough to take a small sip of water she turned around and started for home. A pack of wild dogs yipped and barked in the distance. She mentally picked her return route in a way that would take her by three of her water-traps. If it was safe, she would check their levels and plan a return trip to collect the precious life fluid later, when it was storming.

Nearly two hours had passed and her only company was still the four dead rats. She removed her pack to maneuver through the remnants of a small structure and between two bent, steel I-beams. Climbing over it would have left her too exposed and going around seemed more trouble than it was worth. Halfway through, Sarah was jerked to a stop by a tug on her jeans. Her legs were too confined to kick behind her. Her right hand went back to inspect. A piece of rebar had pierced her jeans like a fishhook, and she was trapped. She struggled to free herself for a few minutes, then stopped instantly. Her left ear had caught sound of something. She remained calm and stone-still. Her senses strained. The lactic acid building up in her quadriceps, hamstrings, and glutes was starting to whisper at her to move.

It was a human voice coupled with footsteps, and it was getting very close. She remained motionless. The burning in her legs was almost unbearable. The sound continued. It made its way past, and away from her. She hoped its originator would keep moving. The noises stopped after a few seconds. The girl felt like puking. Out of nowhere, some strong, unseen force gave her rear-end a brutish push and she was sent sprawling out from beneath the I-beams, surprised and angry. The loosening kick had caused the rebar hook to tear her jeans and gouge her right shin to the bone.

"Boo! Remember me?!"

The rusty voice screeched laughter as she tried to stand up as quick as possible. The man climbed over the ruins to where she was. He was smiling and missing a front tooth. Sarah got to her feet and was starting to run towards cover when something heavy and sharp hit her right calf. She winced, fell to one knee, and saw the broken, jagged brick that had been thrown at her. It had ripped through and torn a chunk of meat out of her calf. She tried to stand but a fierce kick between her shoulder blades sent her flying like a child's toy thrown in a tantrum.

"Ya didn't think I could ever forget ya, did ya, beautiful? It's been a long time and I missed ya. It's too bad my stupid friend isn't here, isn't it? He'd really love to see this. Nevar woulda guessed I'd a found ya all balled up like a present wrapped just for me." The ragged thief spit at her and laughed. Sarah was attempting to catch her breath and think at the same time. She knew the man would not kill her right away. She was too valuable as a woman, for one. And he knew the only way to find the water supply was through her.

She had scrambled onto her back and was trying to stand up. The bandit came up quick and kicked her ankles out from under her. He rushed to stand over her and began grinding his boot into her right wrist. He bent down to pick her up by the collar when she surprised him by throwing a handful of black dirt into his open-eyed face. "Goddamn you!" he yelled and tried to rub his eyes, making it worse. Using her free hand, Sarah quickly unsheathed her knife and forced it into the man's right thigh, twisted it, and pulled it out. Her face showing a snarl of violence for only a second.

"AAHHH...You fucking bitch!" He was livid. The spittle in the corners of his cracked lips rocketed out between gasps. He let one hand drop to clutch his thigh, and in that instant Sarah stabbed into the hand all the way to the leg underneath it. The man sprang off of her wrist and retreated a few steps.

Sarah knew her calf was too hurt to run. She could barely stand on it and it hadn't stopped bleeding. Only the death of this monster guaranteed her escape. Her back had already begun to bruise and stiffen up, and her wrist was likely broken from where the thief had crushed it with his heavy boot. Her shin stung and the gouged skin laid like a flesh ribbon. Overhead, clouds had begun to form.

She still had her knife and her wits, though. The thief slowly regained his composure and had picked up a metal pipe with his good hand. He limped towards Sarah but remained leery.

She crawled backwards and propped herself up on the shell of a burned, rusted truck and waited for his next move. The thief stopped. He squinted through the mud in his eyes and heaved the pipe at her. It was an accurate throw, and her right arm up came up quick to shield her face. The pipe hit with an extremely hard crack as it broke her arm. Sarah almost yelled out but gritted her teeth instead. The agony from her arm spread to her shoulder and neck. Her fingers went numb. She dropped her useless appendage, hung her head, and started to sway.

Sensing she was beyond fighting and forgetting the damage done to his leg, he ran towards her at full speed. She managed to see him through the tears and rolled away just as he crashed head first into the trucks metal skin.

Dazed, he turned slowly. Not wanting to get any closer than she had to, Sarah sheathed her knife and reached out to grab the metal pipe that broke her arm.

"My...turn...now." She wound up and swung hard, aiming for the man's temple. It struck on the right side, making a grotesque popping noise. The thief's eyes rolled backwards and he slumped to his knees. Sarah swung the pipe harder, towards the same spot, and connected once more. The sound was softer this time, but no less brutal. The man started to make mumbling noises but refused to topple over. His eyes had started bouncing in their sockets and his dirty fingers were convulsing. Drool started to fall from his half-closed lips and his right ear was oozing blood and other semi-solid substances. She gathered strength from a reserve deep inside her and swung one more time with all she had left. The pipe embedded itself into the side of his head with a dull slap, as if it had been smashed into a mound of clay. She let the pipe go and stumbled back a few paces. He slowly let out one last breath then fell forward like a rotten tree-trunk, the pipe popping out of his head as he hit the ground.

"Hard-headed bastard..." she said, sitting. She was lightheaded and exhausted. Her calf had been painting the ground red this whole time. Her entire body hurt. She tried to think. She was broken and barely alive. She grabbed for her water but realized she had lost it in the fight. She sighed. A chill began growing inside of her. The pain in her arm had become an annoying numbness. Her calf had ceased to exist. Her shin was forgotten.

The wind had picked up. It ripped around the ruins of the burnt city, but no longer sounded tortured. The night's darkness embraced her. The clouds retreated from each other to reveal a sky full of constellations, as if in final offering. Sarah looked up. She took one last look at the stars that had guided her way many times. They looked closer and brighter than ever. "There's Mars," she whispered to herself, and smiled. She shivered, and gasped. Her body fell backwards. The stars faded to black. Sarah's eyelids fluttered, and then closed.

❧

Francisco J. Ibanez *spent the majority of his life growing up in Liberal, Kansas before moving to Portland, Oregon in 2005. He enjoys skateboarding, reading, hiking, and exploring the outdoors in different ways whenever he can. He's always been intrigued (and terrified) by the not so far-fetched idea of trying to survive and live on a post-apocalyptic Earth. Currently, he's enrolled at Portland Community College with the goal of transferring to Portland State University and becoming a middle school science teacher.*

Francisco would like to thank fellow author James B. Pepe for his guidance and feedback while writing this story.

WOLF MOTHER

MARIE CALHOUN

Thistles do not bother me as I walk, burrs in my fur do not worry me as I walk down the mountain pass. I have been called back from the mountaintops and the swamps, called back from the deep valleys and the dark woods, called away from my dens in the Sahara and the artic.

I was a memory once, setting one foot down in the fall leaves, a paw in the cold snow of winter, the click of claws on the newly wet stones of spring, and soft pads in the hot dust of summer. I was a memory, a notion, a part of the whole earth, happy in what I was doing when I remembered what happiness was. Yet I have been called back when memory and reality caught hold I remembered those like me and those close to me. They spoke the words that tore my heart, "The Stag Lord is dead!" So here, I am stalking down the mountain passes, loping towards the messenger that will meet me and greet me. The one who will take me back to those under my rule, so I can put the world to right.

ᚼ

I can hear their complaints over and over again in my mind. "They drove us too far; they took all the water and the land. Their killing us." I looked at all of them incandescent eyes glowing in the fire light and said to their whimpers and wails, "I saw it myself, I knew it once, I told them it would happen, but they wouldn't listen to me!"

"Please mother," said the young domesticated slave. "Memory is long but what you speak of is time out of mind."

I looked at the young slave and said, "Yes Rochester III that is true it has been long since the cold ruled the world."

Those most like me nodded their heads in acknowledgement.

"Civilization should never have been allowed to arise," said a croaking voice in the back, "Better they should have been sent scattering back up to the trees where they came from."

"Yet civilization did occur," I said, "by fire and stone, by plough and wheel. They took ax to the forests and used to wood to build dams. I see your people have done quite well for themselves Old Toad in the safe harbors and still waters.

He said nothing then and I spoke again before the others could start. "It is as I said I've seen it before and my warning has gone unheeded. Stag Lord sacrificed himself to save you and it didn't work. Now I have come in his stead. Are there any others who wish to argue the particulars of their creation or will someone give me suggestions on how to handle this."

Most of the animals that met my eye hung their heads and only the young slaves before me looked me in the eye, "And what do you have to say young Rodney?"

The black kitten purred all the louder for his new name and said, "Wolf Mover. Whatever you choose you must choose quickly. I heard the word contagion from those last few hunters who returned from the woods. They are sick at their plow and sick of their work. They can only eat from cans now. And on the night Master Crimson rescued me I heard the men speaking of all out extermination."

It's not like I hadn't heard this all before, these were just words for those who remembered being warm and safe in human company and wanted them to be treated with leniency.

"Outrage after outrage has been visited upon us," I said. Now is the time to make them pay. The intermediary has been killed and there can be no peace. Come Master Crimson we have battle plans to make."

☙

I came down from the mountains and walked softly through the first fields, our fields, not theirs. These are the natural fields where the woods are thick and the deer graze their young fawns on the first green shoots of spring. These are the fields where dens can be made under the gentle loam of the earth, so a pack's alpha female can pup for the first time. These are fields that only know wild poppies and thyme, not the steel point of a plow steered by a horses bit. It was in one of our fields that I met him.

"Wolf Mother," he said.

"Yes I am the Wolf Mother," I said sitting back on my haunches. "I expected one like me or one of those close to me to come."

"Forgive me Wolf Mother," said the male curling his long fluffy tail around his feet and bowing his head to the earth floor. "Our wolves are needed to protect our borders and the dogs. Well they do not wish to meet lest they offend you with their ancestry."

I laughed at this, "It is natural enough for us to breed. It should be no different if the humans picked out particular traits they wished to see dominate. Humans have always had a force in shaping nature like every creature this earth does. It only matters if the dogs can survive now?"

"They do more or less," he said.

"And what is your name fox?" I asked.

"Crimson," said the red and white masked face.

"Then let us go Master Crimson for you have much to tell me and time is growing short."

He led the way from this high air place and led me through the densely packed forests and glades where the animals waited. In sparsely tree littered areas and along blank walks of rock, he told me the lay of the land. Our only constant companion was the hawk and the dove that both flew high to look for trouble and tell of our coming. There were other animals along the way, but their timidity kept them silent and in awe.

"We existed in the fields and in the woods," he began, "but now they exist there. Long had some of our homes been in the waters, the air, along the curves of the river and in the cool damp muddy places, but now they exist their too. They settled the land with steel and stone putting towers in the air and dams across the river. They dug out our cool homes for basements and took over our fields for agriculture. They even re-routed the free form of the river into a useful purpose as canals for their crops," he stopped and took a breath as we rested on a mountain cliff which over looked a deep valley. The sheer mountain face was above us with the tree line of spruce and fir that marched down the slopes, until the annuals of oak, elder, and aspen melted into the valley floor, or at least they used too. I could see a clear valley down there with a multitude of lights skating along the lines of a thin river. Further out were the suburbs with a few houses and trees and then country with fast tracts of farmland that sometimes cut right up to the pine trees. Above the valley far to the north of us was the dam that held back the roaring waters of the river and drowned the valley behind it, which I had known so long ago.

"What of the Stag Lord?" I asked.

"He is dead mother. You know that or else you wouldn't have come."

I waited in silence.

He turned to face me, "Of course you would have come mother I am sorry. It is just too hard when all hope is lost."

"Hope is not lost Master Crimson. The wolves and the dogs knew how to call me and if they had not been here then it would have been up to the lynx and cats," I said.

He bowed his head again and said, "We are not truly sure how it happened mother. He must have been called in spirit by one of them. He was found near a hunters blind with an arrow through the heart and neck. The wolves and stags found the hunter nearby ready to dress the meat, he didn't live long."

"I'm sure he didn't," I said.

"We brought his body back to a clearing he loved. The one I shall take you too shortly. The beavers, badgers, and burrowing creatures raised a cairn for him out the wood, earth, and stone," he said.

"Probably the only worthy construction," I said looking at the valley again.

"Do not blame him mother," Crimson said speaking up. "He thought that man would go back as it always did. In fact, they've started to recede already. All those farm houses are not full and the fields have laid fallow these two years. Some of the slaves say the humans can't grow anything now."

"She'll take it back," I said giving one last glance to the human structures. "Tell me everything that has happened Master Crimson leave out no details." I led the way now, remembering the many paths of the earth.

He spoke of times before and things happened, as I knew they would.

"We lived with them in peace for a short time," she said. "There was plenty of land grazing and foraging for all even hunting for the meat eaters. We did not notice the losses in the very beginning. The change over the humans came slowly enough first one small homestead and then a settlement we could stand, but then they just kept coming. Multiplying over the face of our land pushing us back from the verdant fields into the woods, until they started clearing and mining. Then we were pushed to the wastes, which are mostly swamps and uninhabitable for us."

"Which is where I came from," I said interrupting him.

"Yes mother," he said folding his ears back in contrition.

"Life began in the wastes Master Crimson it is only in the harshest times that we need to return there to remember the past," I said.

The fox picked up his thoughts as we moved swiftly down the mountain ridges.

"Mother we've lost contact with large sections of our friends and families. We've had to be content to sit and wait. It was about this time we noted the slaves that the humans had brought with them to toil the earth were slowly dying for want of relief and compassion. Then a day came when there were very few slaves Mother and that's when they came into the wastes to take our friends and neighbors. They took the boars for their swine, the wood pigeon, and quail for their poultry, and the deer for their red meat. We heard them in the wastes they said they needed food Mother," said the fox.

"They've likely poisoned themselves," I said.

"There are slaves you should talk to mother," he said in a whisper, "and some of our people have returned with word of the human state.

We had entered the clearing and all was solemn and quiet here. I looked instantly for the great set of horns, but only found a pile of earth and wood. I ran over to the cairn and began digging furiously between the stones. Crimson could only whine and come as close as he dared. Just as I was reaching the stench of death, I heard a roaring in the woods. A call of confrontation I had heard often in the years of the rut. A magnificent stag came bursting from the woods with nine-point horns and a coat of dark brown and a chest of bright red. He led other stags behind him followed by the yearlings along with the does and their fawns.

"Is it not enough for you," said the red hart, "can't you be satisfied. You may take anyone of us even I. Just leave our honored dead alone."

I turned to Crimson who explained, "For now we have agreed to only eat the dead."

From behind us, the way he and I had come came a chorus of wolves and the sharper barks of dogs. They came spilling out of the woods multiple packs melded into one led by an alpha and his pregnant dog bitch. "There is to be no fighting here," said the alpha.

"You're not supposed to be feeding here," said the stag.

The wolf did not answer he had seen me and dropped his head to the ground. "Mother," he said. The other wolves and dogs under him murmured my name.

"The wolf mother?" asked the stag.

"Forgive me," he said, "we knew you were coming…"

I filled in the words that he could not say, "but you wanted to protect your honored dead. That is well," I said feeling his horn beneath a loose screen of dirt. "I am satisfied." I left the mound and sat down at its base with Crimson before me, the deer lord to my right and the wolves to the left. "Go out into woods," I said, "And bring only the lords of the forest. We have much to discuss before the general populace will be allowed here."

The animals melted away and I was left alone to mourn a little bit.

 C3

The leaders of animals gathered around the Stag Lord's cairn with mewling, grunts, and barks. They listened as I called for silence. "Is there any here," I asked, "that thinks what is about to happen should not?"

There was agreement in silence except for the raspy breathing of a watery voice, "Mother?" he asked for attention.

"Yes, Old Croak," I said using the generic term.

"Why not the unicorn?" he asked.

"The last unicorn," I said, "has come and gone. It was up to me to be called back into the world again."

The toad gave a harrumph and I looked to the audience at large. "Much has passed from the world," I said, "and men have grown strong, but it is not up to them to rule the world. Is there any disagreement that action should be taken against the races of men?"

This time the silence was met with the watery pop of the frog's ribbit.

"Yes Hopper," I said.

"There are reparations to be made mother, not all of nature's children wish to see humans done away with," said the deep bass voice.

His announcement was met with a trumpet of shrieks and cries, much growling was pronounced with open mouths and heads were lowered with rounded and pointed horns aimed at the amphibians.

"Save it for discussion," I announced.

"Yes discussion, discussion," yelled the frog trying to save his own legs.

"Well then," I said as the animals quieted down, "You Old Croak will go about to all the animals and gather whose opinions are wanted to be heard."

"Yes," said the frog, "we wouldn't want it known that you had led us blindly into battle Mother," he added as an afterthought.

"Then you will help him Hopper. You have until midnight to gather as many animals as you can," I said.

"That is not enough…," began Old Croak.

"I have spoken," I said barring my teeth.

The animals began to disassemble to have council with their own people. I turned to the fox, "Master Crimson go on a slow search and bring those of whom you feel need to be here tonight. I want to hear from your witnesses an hour before the last meeting."

"Yes Mother," he said bowing his head and the white tipped tail frisked off into the darkness.

The valley was almost empty and I turned to contemplate the cairn again.

"You cannot do this alone," said a voice from the past.

"You would choose this burden," I asked the red-hearted stag.

"He was one of the sires of my people," said the stag looking over his shoulder to the few that waited on him.

"And your children?" I asked.

"A male can have many fawns," he said. "It is just my burden to have seen them all taken away in the hunt and by disease."

I walked up to the cairn and uncovered the hidden horn. "In times of warmth the Stag Lord leaps through the woods. In times of cold I stalk through the forest."

"Wolf Mother," he said, "it is still a time of warmth."

"And he is dead," I said bitterly.

"Do not let grief blind you mother. We need both of you in the world to recreate it. Warmth and cold, light and dark must come together to set the world to rites."

"Are you sure?" I asked.

He looked to his people in a last good bye and climbed up to the cairn. He stood before me and let out his warm breath under the pale moon light. He looked up to the sky and then to me with his chin held high and said, "I'm sure."

"My love," I said and he didn't flinch as I tore his throat out.

The wolves howled at this ancient act and the deer frisked and jumped, but they did not run away, because they knew the hunt would have been on.

I left him on the hilltop with his glazed eyes looking into the sky and the horn of his predecessors sticking in his neck. I licked the blood from my muzzle and told the wolves, "Gather all the wood you can find." They went immediately and I turned to the deer and said, "Bring seed spawn and flax, any tinder to start a fire." The animals needed little encouragement and bounded into the woods in a near panic.

Shortly the materials were gathered and fox returned to the clearing along with the squeaks and cries of his witnesses politely out of sight. "What have you done?" he asked in a worried voice as he scented the air.

"What I was asked to do," I said with assurance. "Now I need you to do as I bid you messenger. Do as your forbearer did and bring fire into the world."

He looked at me blankly and asked, "What message will this send to the humans?"

"They will learn to fear," I said.

❦

"I know that some of you say there are good things that the humans can do. Their cleared fields give grain to the birds and vegetables to the browsing animals. Their abandoned sights make good homes for the rearing of young and assure a safe place for winter hibernation. Yet these are not the things nature has given you, but the results of manipulation on a massive scale with the ax, plow, and wheel. These are things we can do on our own with what nature has provided us. We know how to forage in the wild and can make a safe place for our children to be born and always we use tooth, horn, beak, and claw to defend our young.

"I am asked to spare some of those down in the valley who have shown compassion to the slaves. Well I promise you there shall be none," I said pacing the lowering flames of the fire.

"The Stag Lord has been killed and all that is left is savagery. Let the word be spread far and wide that if only the youngest are found alive they are to be brought to me. We shall keep a tighter control on them this time."

I spoke my words to the crowd before the burning cairn. Word had gone out on bird and wing and all had gathered here. Closed and cloven hoof, bristle and tusk, and padded leather claws had joined us. The lynx and bear are few now but those we have I was grateful for. The waning gibbous moon was low in the west and the dawn sun was about to pierce the sky. Dawn it had been whispered over and over again that was when we would retake our lands. When the sun was free from the horizon, we would slip across the edge of the silent fields.

"Dawn is coming," I announced from the ranks.

The wolves my captains and lieutenants and their gentled brothers formed into the main charging body, while the nimble and swift-footed deer would stand on the sides of the infantry. Both wolf and deer knew what had been done and none spoke it beyond their species. The fox stood at my side with the kitten on his back. The maker of fire had known and he hadn't spoken. Then with the first blazing rays of sunlight across the glade, there was a rending crack from the cairn and the flames blazed higher. All the animals balked even those that had had some part. The glade filled with more sunlight and the Stag Lord walked out of the swirling embers.

The animals let out a collective gasp and Old Croak spoke in unbelief, "How can this be?" he asked.

Stag Lord looked at the toad with his golden eyes. There was a loud pop. Below the gasps of disgust from the nearby animals was the quick and whispered voice of Hopper's wife telling him to keep his mouth shut.

The Stag Lord looked at me his golden eyes beneath his beautiful 9-point horns. The coat was the color of gold as I remembered it and there was melding as a distinct red color had settled on his chest. "Savagery tempered with civility," he said. "Revenge at its utmost with a quick dispatch of life."

"Night and day," I said, "cold and warmth to make a better world."

"I'm sure we would agree," he said.

My tall head reached his shoulder and his mighty rack of horns turned to our people, "To arms" he said, "to fight, to wipe out this blight on our path."

I took the lead along with my prong horned stag and we covered the short distance to the edge of the fields. There was only a scenting of the wind to know our people were ready and the humans were afraid. The Stag Lord called out his bellow and I let out my howl. We tore down the signs that would have destroyed us. Those words are bitten, clawed, and pissed upon, but the domestics read them to us before we marched. They said *Open Season*.

Oh, there was blood and pain that day. We brought mayhem to their houses and farms, disorder to their tall buildings and canals. Crimson and his people used their knowledge to start fires and only the human dwellings and fields were destroyed. At the end of the light day, beaver and water animals breached the canal, so the human structures would be totally destroyed. Our losses were light with only the bravest of the wolves and deer perishing. It was a sacrifice to nature. On their side all, the humans were destroyed and there had only been old and middle aged no children were found. For my part, I sent out death squadrons in the darkness of night made up of domestic dogs to sniff out their former masters who had fled. Stag Lord was happiest when the river broke and had washed away the blight. I was happiest when the alpha bitch brought me two whelps in a basket. I did not dare ask where she had found them, fearing she had known them before.

The twin boy and girl I have named Rhonda and Remus, and suckle them at my teat. Stag Lord is proud at what they will become and I already have begun to tell them stories in our glade by the warm embers of a dying fire. They shall hear of horse and wild beast cave paintings in Las Ceaux, about the woman of many breasts in Athens, and especially about the shaman with his hands raised as a rabbit and one foot lifted in dance. He had looked at us in the past in wonder and we had looked back in appreciation at his stag horned head and wolf fur covered back.

ↈ

Marie Calhoun's *family stories have revolved around "what if" questions and their possible outcomes. An early fascination with fantasy, sci-fi, and horror made an impression on her life. She has a M.Ed. in special education and works as a Resource Teacher. She lives in Phoenix, AZ with five cats and a crazy German Shepherd. Her hobbies include reading, patio gardening, and traveling around the desert south-west.*

SEVEN DRABBLES OF THE APOCALYPSE

A. W. GIFFORD

First Seal: *Conquest*

After all the hype and countless ads, the long anticipated Election Day has arrived. Records are broken as hoards of people go to the polls to vote for the young, charismatic politician. Few people see though the veil to the man's true agenda beyond, but like Casandra, no one believes them.

As the votes are counted it becomes clear that no recount will be necessary. This time there are no hanging or dimpled chads to count. The charismatic politician wins the election by the largest margin in history.

It's not until later that a majority of voters regret their vote.

Second Seal: *War*

Despite the promise of World Peace, the new leader launches an attack against the nation's enemies. Men are costly, so the decision is made to let the missiles fly. A retaliatory strike follows even before the first missiles find their targets. Major cities burn; men, woman and children scream. Another volley follows the first, causing even more screaming in secondary cities.

In bunkers, men congratulate themselves on a job well done. As they feast, the Leader stands, raises a glass and proposes a toast,

"Here's to the beginning of the New World Order!" All drink, but only a few cheer.

Third Seal: *Famine*

The dust of war swirls in the air blotting out the sun. Crops fail, livestock die and fish rot along the shoreline of all the oceans, every sea.

The starving masses roam the charred cities looking for food in the piles of ash, eating what they can. Many contemplate the unthinkable when they see fellow scavengers. When your children are hungry you'll consider any and all options to fill their bellies.

The Leader and his compatriots, sit down to a lavish meal of meat, bread and olive oil. Wine flows like blood from an open wounds and the Leader laughs.

Fourth Seal: *Death*

The smoke clears, civilizations lay in ruin. The stench of death—at this moment faint—becomes stronger as the millions of corpses begin to rot in the summer heat. Survivors learn to cope and clean up or they too will face the fate of those that didn't survive.

Disease scampers like a rat around the wasteland and takes a million more the bombs and starvation missed. Now, with the world's population at a sustainable level, the Leader emerges from his hole. The staving masses above, see him as their savior, welcoming the horror of his true agenda with open arms.

Fifth Seal: *Tribulation*

Once again, the sky returns to blue and birds begin to sing. The Leader starts to rebuild the world in his image and all are given a small, white cloth emblazed with the Leaders emblem. With this cloth, food, clothing, shelter and jobs will be given. Without, there is no charity.

A small band of survivors will not give in to the Leaders authority and will not accept his mark. They burn their cloth in public protest. The Leader announces a tribulation and orders all to vow their allegiance to him and those that don't are hunted down like vermin.

Sixth Seal: *Wrath*

The ground begins to shake, mountains crumble, lakes and oceans drain. The earth splits open to swallow the sun. Night falls threatening to never again return.

The Leader's followers scream as their blood fills the streets. The Leader himself goes back into hiding leaving all but a few of his closest followers behind to face the brimstone falling from the sky.

Those that blindly followed the leader, drop to their knees and beg for deliverance while others hide underground like rats, like the Leader. However, nothing will stop the Wrath. Not begging, not doors, not earth, not concrete, not stone.

Seventh Seal: *Final Judgment*

Then silence befalls the land. Those that went into hiding come forth expecting the end has finally arrived. Among them is the Leader, now devoid of his followers. Those that looked to him, now see the errors of their ways and join those that stood in opposition.

"We were fooled!" cry some. "We were blinded!" cry others. Some called for the Leader to be imprisoned while more called for his execution. In the end, the Leader takes his own life. A coward's way out.

Those that stood strong against the leader forgive the others and together they begin to rebuild.

CB

A.W. Gifford an internationally unknown author who gets many of his story ideas from the nightmares of his wife, Jennifer. She too is an author of dark fiction, but she refuses to write her own nightmares as she fears doing so will make them come true. Story ideas also come to him from his dogs, the dust bunnies under the bed and one very helpful garden gnome.

He is the editor at Bête Noire Magazine and Dark Opus Press and his work has appeared in numerous magazines, anthologies and was once spotted stalking the woods of the Pacific Northwest.

He, on the other hand, can be found stalking the woods in the northern suburbs of Detroit, while his wife and daughter huddle in the warmth of the house with their two dogs and the aforementioned dust bunnies.

HIGH ABOVE THE DEAD EARTH

DJ TYRER

In a world without people, you begin to see faces everywhere. Leaves, stains, anything can become a face, a simulacrum of those whom you miss.

The only person CC had left in the world was her mother. She guessed their survival must be due to their genes, as all but a tiny number of people had fallen prey to the virus that had swept around the world. Sometimes, often, she thought it would've been better had they died as well.

The faces that weren't really faces would make CC jump every so often. Her mother hardly ever. Despite the apparent need of the brain to repopulate the world using whatever sets of patterns happened to be handy, the last thing mother and daughter wanted to meet were people. As lonely as they might feel at times, alone and scared, they knew that people were a threat, not their salvation.

CC and her mother had felt differently when the disaster had first begun to unfold. They had imagined that the authorities would look after them and put everything right. The doctors had tried—and died. But, things had quickly fallen apart as people died faster and faster. The survivors fought one another for food and supplies, or anything else that took their fancy, and they had quickly learnt to hide away. Only the deaths of most of the remaining people, from virus or violence, had calmed things, but hadn't removed their fear.

Currently, they were walking along a street between soaring towers that had held offices, but were now humbled and ragged. As fast as the virus had spread and as quickly as it had killed, it had lasted long enough to disrupt deliveries of food and much of what was left had been looted in the final days of panic and chaos. Which meant that as much as the logical course and their natural inclination was to hole up somewhere safe, they had to keep moving in search of food as so many shops and homes had been stripped bare.

"I wish we had a car," sighed CC. She kept her voice low, just in case. It was wishful thinking: there were virtually no cars left in the city and nothing to run them on. Thousands had attempted to flee into the countryside, only to die alone in out of the way places, or trapped in traffic jams on the outskirts of the sprawl.

"Be careful what you wish for," her mother replied.

She was right. They'd seen a taxi driving around, a mangled corpse dragged along behind it.

"Let's try here," CC said.

It was a long shot, but there was always a chance an office building might contain an untouched vending machine. The problem was, all those lower down would definitely have been looted, which meant climbing high—a climb they didn't really have the energy to do. At least this one hadn't been gutted by fire.

The entrance lobby wasn't in too much of a state and only one of the floor-to-ceiling windows was cobwebbed with cracks. Probably because the building wasn't locked up. There was a pair of sliding doors that weren't quite closed. It was a narrow gap, but they could slip through.

Someone had tagged the far wall with yellow paint and, yet again, CC found herself imagining she saw a face. Two swirls connected like eyebrows and below them were dots like eyes. A third swirl was like a nose and an enigmatic smile. Probably some gang had claimed the place as their property as everything went to hell. There had been plenty of gang warfare before the gang members turned on each other or just died.

"Do you think there might still be anyone here?" CC asked her mother.

"No. They're dead or moved on. They'd be in the same boat as us, darling."

"Okay, then," said CC and they headed for the stairs.

Inconveniently, the architect had chosen to place the stairs in the heart of the building, meaning the stairwell was pitch black with the power out; the same reason they couldn't just use the elevators. That did increase the odds that the upper floors had been passed by.

CC and her mother each took out a flashlight, illuminating the stairwell. The stairs went up towards the roof and down into some basement level.

"Up, I guess," CC's Mom said. Her daughter didn't disagree: there was an odd, dank smell coming up from the basement. Possibly it was flooded. With everything breaking down, drains blocking, pumps ceasing to work, basements were beginning to fill with floodwater. Even some of the low-lying streets were underwater.

"Watch your step," she added as they began their climb. Bodies and the mess left by looters could easily cause a fall and a broken leg would be a death sentence. But, the stairs were free of such detritus of the collapse of civilisation, lending them hope they might find food. Looters were seldom tidy.

They stopped at the second floor. There was a vending machine that had been smashed open. The water cooler had been drained. Not for the first time, surveying the computers and other equipment left untouched, CC was struck by the way in which their priorities had changed. Nothing that once had mattered, mattered anymore.

Even the sanitary products in the bathrooms had been looted.

The next floor didn't have a vending machine at the one above that had been looted, too. Still, they were hopeful the higher floors would be untouched.

Mom paused to catch her breath.

"Maybe we can move in. These stairs are killing me." Her attempted jollity was too fragile to carry real conviction.

"Break's over," said CC. "Time to get moving."

The next floor also lacked a vending machine – apparently they alternated floors.

"Hopefully, nobody went much higher," CC's Mom said.

Unfortunately, they had. The next floor had also been cleared out. As had the vending machine two floors above that.

Allowing her mother to take another rest break, CC said, "I don't think we should give up. I reckon the furthest anyone will have gone is ten floors. Beyond that we should be okay."

"Or, dead."

Sitting in the darkness with just a torch for illumination reminded CC of telling ghost stories at camp. That seemed like a different life now.

"Maybe we should spend the night here," she told her mother. "We could find an office with a door and shove a desk up against it. We probably wouldn't even need to, really; nobody is likely to come up this far. At least, not as long as we didn't show any light."

The lights had long since gone out when the power failed. Barring a few lights charged by solar energy during the day, the presence of a light at night meant people and, to some survivors, people meant prey. Allowing a light to show was no longer a good idea.

They continued slowly upward and, on the twelfth floor, hit the jackpot: a vending machine with candy and another with snacks, plus a third with drinks, and a water cooler. There was even a storeroom that contained replacement bottles of water.

"Not too healthy," Mom said, "but, it'll do." She'd always been a stickler for CC eating right. CC had used to resent her fastidiousness, but found she missed fruit, veg and proper home-cooked meals. Despite childhood fantasies, a diet of candy and chips really wasn't fun after a while. Still, it was better than starving.

CC was interested in the water, gulping down paper cup after paper cup.

Water was the problem. Water you could safely drink was a rarity. Finding a bonanza of bottles was great, except for the fact they weren't exactly portable. Shopping carts and such like were easy enough to come by, but you were still limited as to how much you could actually haul about. Though, if they could make a few more finds like this, maybe they could stay put awhile.

"We should keep going," her mother said, after they'd eaten and drunk. "Check a few more floors before nightfall."

It was already growing dark outside.

"Okay, but I'd rather store all this securely so no-one else can take it." She still hadn't quite got away from the irony of worrying about someone looting what they'd worked hard to loot.

"Well, we can't lock it up."

"I know, Mom, but maybe we could put it in an office. That way if anyone else looks in here, they'll see the vending machines are empty and, hopefully, assume there's nothing worth searching for."

Her Mom nodded. They found an office a distance from the stairs and hauled it all in there.

"We could make this our bedroom," CC said, "if we have the energy to come down again."

They set off up the stairs, once more.

CC swore. Her mother had long since ceased to correct her. Her flashlight had begun to dull. Not what you wanted to happen in a pitch-black stairwell. They paused and she shook it, hoping to get the beam back to strength. It didn't work.

"Hang on," Mom said, shushing her.

"What?" CC mouthed at her.

Her mother cupped and ear and nodded downward.

CC listened carefully. There was a sound below them on the stairs. At first, it was a wet sound as if something were hauling itself out of the flooded basement, then a sort of slithering as if something were crawling up the stairs. A slow, deliberate sound.

"What is it?" whispered CC.

"How should I know?" her mother hissed back.

"I think it knows we're here. What do we do?"

"We can't go down?"

"We could barricade ourselves in that office."

Her Mom shook her head. "Then what?"

"Okay, we go up, then. Hope it loses interest."

It. Somehow they knew it wasn't a person. Since the human race had died, animals had become as dangerous as the human predators that remained. But, somehow, they knew it wasn't a pack of rats or rabid dogs or anything like that. It was something else.

They started going up as fast as they could. CC's flashlight was dying and her Mom's had begun to flicker.

Mom swore. She never swore before everyone died.

Suddenly, a light shone down at them, dazzling them and a voice said, "Up the stairs, quick!"

They could barely make out the shape of a figure behind the glare.

Fearing the sounds echoing up from below more, they did as they were told. They were almost at the top of the building, they realised. A couple more floors and the stairs ended at a door.

A man in riot gear, clutching a shield and baton, stood beside the door, his face invisible behind the helmet's visor. He nodded them through the door, which bore the same tag they'd seen in the lobby. For a moment, the tag seemed to reflect in his visor like a face, but then his head had turned back to look down the stairs and it was blank again.

CC pushed the door open and found herself in vast open space, a huge open-plan office. Her mother stumbled in behind her and the shadowy figure that carried an old-style storm lantern followed them in. The man in riot gear stayed outside on guard.

Their guide doused the storm lantern. The day was growing dark: the bloated red sun was sinking behind soaring towers that had once housed the engines of the economy but were now as dead as the people who once had worked there. The sun reflected in the glass as if there were a second bloody sun slowly sinking in the west. There might as well have been two suns in the sky and they might as well have been on an alien world, for the world now was alien to the one they'd once known.

"Who are you?" CC demanded. "And, what was that thing in the stairwell?"

"My name is Yhtill and I am the Guide. That below is something of which I do not speak."

Before she could speak again, there was a voice from elsewhere in the room.

"Welcome to my domain."

The sun had disappeared and only the merest phantom of light remained. They could just make out the silhouette of a figure at the far end of the space.

"Who are you?" CC asked. Her mother seemed too exhausted to do anything.

"I am the One Whom You Seek."

"We aren't seeking anyone," CC's Mom managed to gasp.

"You have followed the Guide. You have passed the Gatekeeper. You have come hence. You have sought me and you have found me."

He stepped nearer. He was dressed in a tattered great coat, like a bum, and his face was pale and skull-like. CC couldn't tell if he wore a mask or if his flesh had been eaten away. The suggestiveness of it made the chips she'd earlier eaten lurch in her stomach.

"But, who are you?" CC's Mom asked.

"You ask, but have yet to introduce yourselves," the man who called himself Yhtill said.

"Um, my name is Sylvia, Sylvia Castaigne. This is my daughter, Constance. Everyone calls her CC."

"Destiny," the man in the mask whispered.

"Sorry? I don't understand."

"You were destined to come here, high above the dead earth, you and your daughter, eve since the day of your births. Everything that has happened has happened for you."

"What do you mean?" CC felt her blood chill.

"My servants set forth into the world to spread the plague to clear it of the unworthy. Only those with the blood of the True Americans could survive. And, of them, only the chosen few could make it here to my court. Here you shall dwell, Queens over the dead earth below."

"You're mad," whispered CC's Mom, backing away, voice quavering.

"Not mad—genius!" said Yhtill, with the delighted voice of a fanatic.

"I cleared this world for you," the man said. "Purged it of all its flaws, all the people that made it such a mess."

"Purged it of the people who made it worth living for," Mom sobbed. Her retreat was halted just before the door where the man in riot gear had stepped through and caught hold of her as she collapsed.

CC looked from the broken form of her mother, to the man with the skull face, the beggar king of a dead world.

"I made this world for you," he said. "Join me."

CC thought of the life they'd led since everyone had died: a futile-seeming struggle to stay alive in a world which offered no reason to live. A life of looted snack food. Here, it seemed, her existence in this strange and terrible world would be given meaning. This was her destiny.

"I'll join you," CC said.

Behind her, her mother sobbed.

CC gazed up at the blank face of the man and saw that the peculiar symbol seemed now to be upon him, providing an illusion of a face where none was.

In a world without people, CC thought, you began to see faces everywhere, even here. Had they really found the architect of the lifeless world or did they imagine faces where there were none in a desperate quest for company and to impose order upon the chaos?

She suppressed such thoughts and stepped forward to reject her past and embrace her future.

She would rule here, forever more, high above the dead earth. A faceless queen in a faceless world.

ॐ

DJ Tyrer *is the person behind Atlantean Publishing and has been widely published in anthologies and magazines in the UK, USA and elsewhere, most recently in* Amok! *(April Moon Books),* State of Horror: Illinois *(Charon Coin Press),* Steampunk Cthulhu *(Chaosium),* Tales of the Dark Arts *(Hazardous Press) and* Cosmic Horror *(Dark Hall Press), and, has a novella available on the Kindle,* The Yellow House *(Dynatox Ministries).*

COLONY COLLAPSE

SUSAN NANCE CARHART

The scout returned in a humming of wings. The Queen waited for the report, hoping for the best, expecting the worst. Rumors and speculation were seething throughout the hive. Her subjects were afraid. Here in the Great Chamber of her realm, life seemed as smooth and industrious as ever, as diligent workers processed food and tended the young. In the great world outside, however, things had changed. The Queen wanted a clear understanding of what they were dealing with.

She did not have long to wait.

"The South Colony is...abandoned," said the exhausted scout.

The worst, then.

"Tell me everything."

The scout did, with scrupulous care. Their kind did not so much speak in words as express themselves in dance-like movements, subtle and elegant. The scout, Zzon124, managed to combine respect and reverence for the Queen with admirable precision and clarity in describing the events.

"There were no guards at the entrance. There was no one to be found in any of the passages. The Great Chamber was empty but for the Queen, the former Lady Apis. She had been dead for some time."

The Queen tried to imagine it, guessing that the scout, out of concern for her feelings, was not sharing the most distressing details. Having heard other reports like this, the Queen could almost smell the odor of death and abandonment; feel the old, crumbling wax underfoot; see the shriveled, dried-up husk of one who had once been vital and beautiful. It was a grief to her: she pictured Lady Apis' great dark eyes dulled by dust; her hair filthy and untended. And there was worse news yet.

The scout hesitated. "She was alone, but…"

"But…?"

"But for the nursery…" Zzon124 trembled, mandibles clicking nervously. "The young were left sealed in. None survived."

A long silence. The Queen was perfectly still. Yes, this fit in with the rumors and gossip. Brief, haphazard encounters with strangers from distant colonies warned of disaster, of contagion and apocalypse moving steadily in their direction. The catastrophe left hives empty but of dead queens and the sealed-in young. What was the cause? What could they do?

Some blamed the gossiping strangers themselves, saying they carried disease; some believed the strangers' talk of a failing food supply; some wondered about the curious disappearance of plant life in the area. Some even complained about the nectar that the gatherers had brought in recently: that some of it was *different,* somehow; different and bad.

Young firebrands like Lady Bez thought the big scavengers were responsible: the giant, bizarre, four-legged creatures that walked on two legs and used their upper two legs for food-gathering and aggression. It was they, she said, who spread disease when they attacked and looted hives.

The Queen kept her posture strong and fearless, though she was struggling against paralyzing dread and an aching sense of loss. Lady Apis had been brave and lovely, and the Queen had been proud of her. Lady Bez, on the other hand, had always been the most difficult of her daughters. Things were already bad, but Bez was bound to make things worse by creating a violent scene.

Here she was now, bursting in with scandalous aggression, invading what was a private conversation.

"Is it true?" Bez demanded. She was trembling; antennae flicking ominously. "Are they all dead? Apis and all the others?"

The scout backed away, trying to become inconspicuous. Bez could be overwhelming, even in a good mood. Now she was dangerous. The Queen had been looking forward to Bez's ultimate departure ever since she left the nursery.

Whatever was happening, starting a panic would not help. The Queen moved forward, her posture as dominant as she could make it. She was still a little larger than her young daughter, and tried to use her size to her advantage.

"We don't know that they're dead, Bez," she said, trying to imagine some way in which some of the colony might have survived. "They're *gone.* We don't know what happened to them. Apis is dead, yes: and the young. The rest abandoned the hive."

Bez only trembled the more, each hair on her sleek, striped body vibrating. Her scent changed; turned bright and sharp. The Queen braced herself for an outright attack. It would be unfortunate if she was forced to kill Bez, but she would do it for the greater good. At the worst, she would summon her subjects to surround Bez. If they swarmed long enough in one place, they could raise the temperature to lethal levels. Instead, she decided to hear her out. Bez was rash, not stupid. She was frightened now, but that was unsurprising. The Queen was frightened herself; her mind fluttering like a damaged wing as she tried to plan defenses against an unknown, overwhelming peril.

Bez danced out her thoughts in abrupt, jerky steps; each movement a testament to her growing anxiety.

"That's how it always happens! That's what the stories describe! Apis alone, the nursery cells capped...everyone else gone. We've got to get away!"

The possibility of flight had already crossed the Queen's mind. Each frightening rumor made her consider it again. Each time she thought of it, she rejected it. Her realm was dear to her: the place she had discovered long ago on that great, delirious flight through flowery meadows and cool forests with her mates and loyal retainers by her side. Here they had built something of value: a place of shelter and comfort, sweet-scented and orderly. Here her children had come into the world. Every hall, every chamber, every six-sided cell held meaning for her. Nothing in her nature made abandoning her hive an acceptable choice. She stood strong, making explicit her determination.

"This is our home. You, of course, could go. If these were ordinary times, you would be leaving soon with the young drones, anyway."

"No!" Bez inched forward, ready to lunge. "We must *all* go!"

The Queen did not flinch. "Go where? And for us *all* to go is madness. Do you know what kind of effort it would take to move the entire colony? Do you understand how many of the young would die?"

"Better some of us than all of us!" raged Bez, antennae twitching. "And what about that one?"

Zzon124 shrank away.

"Yes, you! You've been in that diseased place, that dead hive, and you came back here, trying to infect the rest of us. Get out! Get out, before I kill you!"

The Queen moved between Bez and the scout, who took the opportunity to escape.

"The scout did exactly as I told her to. This is not your hive to command, and no one is to be killed on your orders."

Bez turned her great, complex, beautiful eyes toward the Queen. She lowered her head to battle stance.

"Then we need a new hive and a new Queen!"

"You *need* to calm down," said the Queen, restraining her own fear and anger with grim effort. Bez did not understand how close she was to being attacked and killed. The Queen reminded herself that she was the adult here. Bez was only young and irritating, after all, and the Queen did not wish to lose any more children today. "We know very little about what is actually happening. Splitting the hive and putting half in very real danger while trying to establish a new colony may be the *worst* thing we can do."

That gave Bez pause. Her agitated movements slowed, and were tentative and erratic as she worked out her thoughts.

"It's the work of those giants, somehow; those scavengers that walk on two legs. I *know* it. We need to get far away from them!"

"How can it be related to them? Be reasonable. We've never been able to detect any sign of intelligence in them. They're not like ants or termites that show a decent—if inferior—level of organization. As far as we can tell, they are completely unable to communicate in any meaningful way." The Queen made a delicate gesture of distaste. "And they are so *slow*, Bez!"

"But they're *everywhere*." The other female's movements became quicker and more precise. "They build, too: maybe by mere instinct, but we know they can cooperate on some level. They steal honey and ruin hives. You know as well as I do that some of them even live near hives as parasites. You don't have to be intelligent to destroy the world." Bez twitched sharply in laughter. "In fact, being mindless would do as well!"

"But *we* are not mindless," countered the Queen, in an elegant, measured dance step. "We need to assess the danger carefully, and then make our plans. We can't simply panic like animals."

Bez trembled again. "All right. We know that this contagion, whatever it is, is coming this way. It doesn't make sense to wait for it to find us. If I take some of our people—say to the Second North Plum Orchard—then we have a better chance of our people surviving as a whole. The Orchard is remote. None of the two-legged scavengers live nearby, and there are none of the wide strips of black ground ooze they secrete there."

"Apis thought that the South Colony would be safe, too. We don't know what's causing this, Bez. What if it's caused by mites or some other tiny creatures that live on bigger animals? What if dividing our people simply makes it easier for this contagion to destroy them? Perhaps we'd do better to keep scouts posted, with orders to drive away any creatures that approach the hive."

The Queen liked the idea of quarantining the hive the more she thought of it. She wished she had done it long ago. Perhaps it was already too late. Perhaps she had been wrong not to call in the far-roaming scouts at the first warning of danger. Perhaps she herself had already brought destruction on the hive. That thought was too unbearable to dwell on. And Bez was vibrating back and forth in disagreement, anyway.

"Driving away animals means sacrificing scouts. And sometimes stings don't work on the scavengers."

"But usually they do. I once saw one of those creatures die of a single sting. I would rather fight for my home than run away."

Bez seemed calmer now, her movements slower and smoother. The Queen thought she had won the argument, when another scout zoomed in and twitched out an even more alarming report.

"Dead Beech Colony is gone! Empty except for —"

Without even listening to the rest, Bez launched herself at the Queen, her scent heady with anger and the will to rule. Her front legs locked around the older female's body, pinning her down, while she rained down blows with her four rear limbs. Workers in the Great Chamber milled about, alarmed at the sudden battle disrupting their labors.

Taken by surprise, the Queen flailed ineffectually, on her back and terrifyingly vulnerable, twisting to avoid the pummeling. She was trapped, unable to release her pheromones, unable to summon help. She tried to curl up, holding the pain at bay, but Bez's eyes stared into hers, black holes of unleashed rage. Mandibles clicked in her face: impudent, defiant. Another kick. Another savage, thrashing blow. The Queen, dazed and helpless, could only hope it would soon be over.

"We're leaving!" Bez raved. "We're leaving *now!* Stay and die if you like! I'll lead our people to safety!"

Not bothering to finish off her stunned opponent, Bez was up and rushing out of the Great Chamber, her pheromones fierce and commanding, urging them all to follow her. A tremendous thrumming vibrated throughout the hive, the thunder of an angry, frightened swarm, as over half the colony took to the air.

Most of the workers in the Great Chamber obeyed Bez: they were closest, after all. Many in the nursery and the lower chambers answered the summons as well. The young drones, stupid with lust, followed her, too; but that was no more than the Queen expected. The air hummed with single-minded purpose, and bee after bee flew after their chosen leader.

At the congested entrance, there was a frantic din, as the weaker were trampled and smashed by the stronger as they fought to escape. Pitiful twitching forms kept on trying to follow their comrades toward the shining promise of the sunlit entry. Some managed to fly, after a fashion. Others dropped to the mossy tree roots below, and were still.

Once the fugitives were gone, silence closed in. Those remaining — mostly from the upper passages, where the Queen's residual pheromones had dominated — gaped after the vanishing swarm, wondering what to do.

"My Queen, are you hurt?"

Zzon124 crept out of hiding, humble and concerned.

The Queen was not too sure at first, but managed to get all six legs under her. She flicked her wings anxiously.

"Everything works. I suppose I'd better see who's left."

Bewildered grief made her slow. Was this what had happened to the other colonies? She wondered about that as she reassigned workers to the nursery and assessed the damage caused by the abrupt desertion. Was it a real disease, even, or simply mass hysteria? Already she could see doubt in her remaining subjects; lack of faith in her leadership. Would they, too slip away, emptying the hive, leaving her behind to die alone? The hive could still collapse into chaos and death. Everything depended on what she did next.

She pulled herself together, radiating calm and command, releasing her own pheromones. She must have confidence in herself, if the rest were to have confidence in her. Or she must at least pretend confidence, for she truly did not know what was best to do. Perhaps Bez was right to flee. Perhaps she herself was right to stay. Perhaps there was no right answer, and the coming doom would sweep them both away, indifferent to their battle for supremacy.

But she must do *something*. Any decision was better than none at all.

"Zzon124," she said, "gather the scouts. Throw out a protective screen around the hive. Don't permit any outsiders to approach. Kill them if you have to. If animals stray too near us, use deadly force to move them away."

The scout crouched in submission. 'Deadly force' meant her own death, and the death any other scouts who stung the beasts. She accepted this, having always known that someday she might be called upon to give her life for Queen and Hive.

"But what about our own people?" she asked, greatly daring. "What if they come back? Should they be allowed to return?"

The Queen briefly considered that. Would some calm down after Bez's rebellion, and see reason? Or had the young fool led them straight into harm's way?

"No," she decided, her posture composed. "No. Once they are out in the world, they might well bring back whatever it is that is killing us. No. Warn them away. They made their choice, and we made ours. We are on our own. From this moment, we must consider ourselves besieged, and the last bees in the world."

☙

Susan Nance Carhart *has degrees in history and music. Mild-mannered bureaucrat by day and creator of fantastic worlds by night, she picks apart societal and scientific trends and ponders where they might lead. Truth really is stranger than fiction, but she tries to keep up.*

Her stories have appeared in the anthologies Horror, Humor, and Heroes, *volumes two and three, in* Buzzymag, *in the Third Flat Iron anthology* Astronomical Odds, *and in* 365 Tomorrows. *She lives with her books, her harp, and her can-fix-anything husband near Chicago.*

SALVAGE

PATRICK SCALISI

From Caltech's *Science Today! Magazine*, Aug. 29, 2017.

Bringing Asteroids Closer
Most scientists at world space agencies want to keep near-Earth asteroids away from the planet and have spent years developing contingency plans in case a space rock buzzes too close to our home world.

Moon Ki-Yong is not most scientists.

The South Korean expat, whose resume includes work at JAXA and NASA, says it would be relatively easy to place a near-Earth asteroid in orbit around the planet for exploration and mining.

Writing in the September issue of the *American Journal of Space Science*, Moon, who currently works in the private sector for OroCorp (NYSE: OROC), says that he has identified several candidates that could be fired into Earth orbit by changing their velocity.

Doing so should place the selected asteroid in an orbit at about twice the distance of the Moon — virtually our backyard in galactic terms.

 CƷ

It was our second night in the Crash Zone when Serge finally asked the question. We had been circling the topic for two days, like a pair of vultures wheeling over a fresh piece of carrion. Now Serge put down the camp meal he was eating out of a metal plate, looked across our small lantern and asked, "What do you think is on the drive?"

I looked up from my own meal—jerky with some canned beans that I had heated over a battery-powered range—and stared at the mix of light and shadow that covered Serge's face in the autumn night.

I shrugged. "Dunno. Guess it's not really our place to ask."

Serge seemed to accept that. He returned to his meal and took a few more bites. I thought maybe that would be the end of it.

"You gotta wonder, though," Serge continued suddenly, putting his fork down with a clatter. "I mean, the man's the head of one of the biggest tech companies in the world. Wouldn't you wanna look?"

"Want to?" I asked, purposely not looking up again. "Sure. But I won't. That's not our job."

Serge wasn't about to let go of the game so easily: "What's he got on there that's so important? Huh? C'mon Rob, what's on there? Kiddie porn? New product? The president's phone number?" He picked up his fork and jabbed it in my direction. "I bet it's some new gadget. Remember that time—shit, who was it? I think it was some tech journalist got ahold of one of Baker's prototypes. Baker paid a hundred grand to shut him up. Now that's—"

I slammed my fork against the can of beans.

"I—we—are not paid to look at the hard drive; only retrieve it," I said.

I was looking directly into Serge's eyes now and tried not to get distracted by the light from the lantern that was reflected in his pupils. Serge met my gaze for a second, then looked down and to the right.

"Jesus Christ," he said. "Chill the fuck out, okay? We used to do this all the time, remember? 'What's on the encrypted CD? What's in the sealed manila envelope?' Shit, remember that time we had to get those five-and-a-quarter floppies out of Margao? Who the hell would want those?"

"Someone who paid us two hundred and fifty thousand, if I remember."

"Yeah, so now Mister Howard Baker comes to us and offers a million dollars to get a hard drive outta the Crash Zone and you don't even question it?"

I shrugged again. "It *must* be sensitive if he's offering that much. And for that kind of money, I don't need to know."

Serge must have sensed that he had pushed far enough. He retrieved his dinner and shoveled the rest into his mouth. Then he rolled out his sleeping bag without another word. I guess he meant for me to take the first watch, so I grabbed the scanner, turned off the lamp and listened as Serge's breathing steadied into the even rhythm of sleep.

We continued our trek at dawn the next day, hoping to make it to the ruins of Baker's house by late afternoon. We were lucky the job wasn't in the absolute heart of the Crash Zone, which was roughly the size of Connecticut. As it was, the trip would take six days on foot — three days in and three days out, each day boosting our chances of being caught by an air patrol.

Since the Crash Zone was off-limits, you had to be dropped outside the perimeter for a trip into the zone, though the guards on the border were too few to put up any kind of effective watch. That's where the air patrols came in. The little drones were supposed to scan for radiation, but they were the *real* watchers, since the government wasn't letting people back in to get their stuff yet — what was left of it anyway. Everything Serge and I passed looked like the aftermath of an atomic blast: houses bowled over, trees the size of buses uprooted, and concrete roads warped and cracked. Baker had claimed that his basement vault could withstand a nuclear bomb. When I asked if it was rated for an asteroid strike, he had laughed and offered assurances that it was the best that money could buy. In any case, I didn't care if the house was there or not; he was paying for our little weeklong hike regardless.

"Shit — air patrol!" said Serge. He had stopped walking and was staring at the scanner, which was slung around his neck.

For a second, an absurd image came to mind: Serge reminded me of Commander Spock using a tricorder, and the devastated landscape around us was just another planet that he, Kirk and McCoy had come to explore like in the old shows I used to watch with my mother.

I started laughing.

"Rob, did you hear me? Air patrol!"

I saluted and pointed to a nearby plaza with a parking lot and storefronts whose contents had been looted by survivors. The lot was like an automotive killing field. Almost no cars were parked properly in their spaces, and only a few were actually upright. Others had been turned over by the blast, while some, weirdly, were balancing on their sides or in pileups. Oil and gasoline smeared the pavement where they had leaked from their dying owners, stains that would mark for years the number of cars and trucks that had been wrecked when the asteroid hit.

"Hurry up, hurry up!" Serge said as we took shelter under the bed of an overturned pickup truck whose weight was now supported by the cab.

"How long?" I asked.

"Seconds."

As soon as the words left his mouth, we heard a high-pitch hum from somewhere above us. It took another moment for the drone to pass by the thin triangle of sky that we could see from beneath the pickup truck. To me, it looked like some kind of multi-rotored bug with surveillance gear bulging from the belly of its carapace.

Serge exhaled as we waited for the sound to recede.

"How many is that so far?" I asked.

Serge took a felt-tip marker from his pocket and rolled up his left sleeve to reveal a number of hatch marks. He added one to the set.

"Eight," he said. "Let's give it a few minutes."

Serge produced a bottle of water from our pack. He took a drink and passed it to me.

"Still pissy?" he asked while I swallowed.

"What?"

"You. Last night. Never seen you get so uptight about a job before. And anyway, who's gonna hear us guess about what's on the hard drive out here?"

My aggravation from the night before rekindled. "I've seen you get like this before, and on jobs that paid less," I replied, shoving the bottle back into his hands.

"Yeah, but I'm seeing opportunities here that you're not, Rob." Serge capped the bottle and put it back into the bag. Then he checked the scanner again and continued, "Say it is some new product. Something big that's still in R and D. Who's to say we don't copy the drive before giving it back to Baker?"

I shook my head, barely letting him finish. "Stop. Just stop. Baker told me the drive's protected by something that's not even on the market. Copying's out of the question. The man's a genius, so I'm gonna take his word on that. And second, remember that tech journalist you mentioned? Well imagine that's us. But what we're doing here is a lot less public. Maybe Baker doesn't *pay* us to shut up. Maybe we just disappear."

"Pillar of the community, like that? I don't think so. Even if he does have a prickly personality."

"People with money do whatever they want."

Serge consulted the scanner and decided it was safe to venture out from beneath the wreck. Even so, we had to dodge two more air patrols before making it to Baker's house, each time ducking into rubble or an abandoned building to avoid the drones. And each time, Serge added more hatch marks to his arm and looked as if he wanted to argue more about the hard drive. But he kept his mouth shut.

It was late afternoon when the house finally came into sight. It was large, as was to be expected, and certainly outpaced many of the other mansions in a neighborhood that had no shortage of palatial estates.

The main house was set in the center of a massive lot, neglected lawns rolling away in all directions. Where once the grounds might have resembled a putting green, the grass was now overgrown nearly to our knees with wide swaths of yellow and brown weeds choking out the smaller islands of emerald. To the rear of the main estate was a small guesthouse—small, in that it was the size of a normal suburban home and dwarfed in comparison to its deluxe cousin. Between them was an in-ground Olympic-size pool.

Approaching the house from the front, it was possible to think that the building might have escaped significant damage. The front portico, with its two-storey balcony set on marble pillars and backed by a façade of stonework, was completely intact, as were a number of the front windows. It was only when we started up the side lawn that we realized that the rear of the building had taken all of the impact and that, indeed, the guesthouse was leaning to one side.

The rear of the main estate resembled a child's dollhouse: picturesque in the front, with the rear wall exposed so that figurines and miniature furniture could be placed, removed or rearranged during playtime. Serge and I looked up into bedrooms, drawing rooms and a library that took up most of the third storey. All of the rooms had been ravaged by months of exposure to the elements. Papers fluttered whenever the wind blew, while painted walls and furniture showed signs of water damage and animal markings. Glass, wood, shingles and siding were strewn about the back lawn as if a tornado had hit. Wood and plastic debris floated in the pool.

"There." Serge pointed to a set of concrete steps that led down into the building's foundation. With a few hours of daylight left, we grabbed our flashlights and ventured into the cellar to finish our job.

The basement was, surprisingly, unfinished—no billiards room, no wine cellar, no movie theater. There was a fair amount of water on the floor, though, either from a broken pipe or from rain that had run down the exposed stairway. To the left was our ultimate destination.

Set in an otherwise nondescript wall was a vault door like one might see at a bank. Burnished metal flashed in the light of our torches, which also revealed hinges the size of a baby's arm and a turn wheel in the center of the door. On the wall to the right of the vault was a keypad and finger plate, along with an access panel.

A groan reverberated throughout the basement as we stepped off the concrete steps. Serge and I both spun in place, looking for the source of the distress. Several of the load-bearing columns in the basement were warped or cracked, and one was toppled over entirely. The one nearest to the bottom of the staircase seemed to vibrate, but it could have been a trick of the light.

"Let's get this over with," I said in a whisper. "Quietly."

We ventured over to the vault door and set to work.

"The vault's on its own circuit," I said. "Gimme a screwdriver. Take the batteries out of the range."

In a few moments, there was a nest of wires hanging from the access panel, the batteries feeding them power through an inverter. The keypad and finger plate glowed with life; everything was as Baker had described.

Serge removed the scanner from around his neck, placed it inside our bag and rummaged around until he found his battered notebook. Holding the flashlight between his teeth, he skimmed the warped pages, which were filled with his sloppy handwriting. Finally, he came to the one he was looking for, withdrew a thin plastic packet and studied the writing on the ruled page—hieroglyphics that were legible only to him.

"4-9-1-5-3-7," he said through the flashlight in his mouth.

I punched the numbers on the keypad, which flashed green.

"Fifteen seconds for a fingerprint," I said.

Serge dropped the notebook and peeled apart the two halves of the plastic packet to reveal a gel simulacrum of Baker's thumbprint. Then he nearly stumbled over himself to get to the finger plate in time. We only had one copy of Baker's thumbprint, and it would dissolve in a few seconds once exposed to the outside air.

Serge pressed the gel fingerprint to the plate and waited. The window was so narrow that I was afraid we had screwed up, that we would have to return to our client empty-handed.

Then a whole new set of fears sprang up in my chest.

With a basso *thud*, the bolts in the vault door withdrew into their sockets. I shielded my head with one arm, expecting the sound and the vibrations to send the whole house toppling down on top of us. But apart from a few pebbles and a cloud of plaster dust, the basement remained intact.

Serge swore.

"Let's not push our luck," I replied, reaching for the vault door. "Let's get the drive and get the hell outta here."

A single overhead bulb was active inside the vault, apparently tied to the same circuit as the keypad. The light fell on a small, austere room with metal shelves, filing cabinets and safe deposit boxes.

Serge paused to look around greedily. "Oh man, the stuff that's probably in here."

"No time," I replied. "This place doesn't have long."

I used Baker's key to unlock box 19. I opened the security door, removed the box and checked to see that the hard drive was inside. Then I put everything into our bag and shouldered the pack.

"Let's go," I said.

I exited the vault, not bothering to close the door, and made for the stairs that led back into the yard. Every second inside the basement made me more aware of the inexorable weight of the house pressing down on us.

I put my foot on the first step and heard a click echo in the empty basement behind me. I turned to find Serge holding a gun on me.

"We need to get something straight," he said. "I'm not bringing that hard drive to Baker."

Strange as it may sound, I was more worried about being on the threshold of the basement than having a gun pointed at me. My brain failed to process the unreality of the situation: My partner of eleven years was ready to shoot me.

"I mentioned opportunity, Rob, and we both have a chance to make out here," he continued. "OroCorp is offering double what Baker promised us. The product plans on that drive'll help 'em beat the competition for the next decade, if not longer."

"You don't know what's on the drive."

"OroCorp is willing to pay two million to find out. One of their staff got ahold of a secret memo from Baker. He's buying lobbyists to lift the quarantine on the Crash Zone. Said his company has an economic stake here."

I was starting to get angry now, as much at myself as at Serge. He had been hinting at this for days; I don't know why I didn't see it sooner.

"Do we have an understanding?" he pressed.

I stepped back into the basement, closing the gap between Serge's gun and my chest. This seemed to make him less confident, and I saw a flicker of doubt cross his eyes in the dim light streaming from outside.

"You're not gonna shoot me, Serge. And we're not handing this drive over to OroCorp."

I took another step toward Serge, who retreated backward in response. The muzzle of his gun was dipping toward the floor now. I pushed onward.

"I am *not* disappointing a million-dollar client. It would be the end for both of us."

Another step.

Serge started to say something when he backed into one of the load-bearing pillars. I heard a snap, followed by the loudest groan yet and a shower of building materials. I didn't wait. I turned and raced toward the basement stairs, not bothering to look behind me. There may have been a gunshot in the ruckus, but if there was, it was overtaken by the noise of the house collapsing. I just ran.

It was only later, after I had emerged from the cloud of dust and sprinted across the estate grounds, that I noticed Serge wasn't behind me.

CB

Howard Baker was in the process of firing someone when I arrived at his office; he didn't make any attempt to hide what was happening.

"Han, your carelessness just doesn't align with the design aesthetics of this company," Baker was saying in a raised tone. He smacked a few papers on his desk with the back of his hand. "If I've told you once, I've told you a hundred times: inelegance has no home here. Pack up your things. I'm sure your services will be needed elsewhere."

The cowed employee, an Asian man, made no attempt to argue. He scooped up the papers that Baker had so easily dismissed and stomped from the office.

Baker turned to me without missing a beat. "Tell me you got it," he said in the same agitated tone. "I don't think I can handle any more bad news today."

Without a word, I placed an attaché case on his desk and opened it. The interior had been modified with molded padding to hold the hard drive.

Baker's face changed instantly. Gone were the stress and worries of his company, but at the same time, he seemed to age ten years right before my eyes. I noticed the purple bags under his eyes, the way his shoulders stooped. He breathed a sigh of relief.

"Thank you," he said. "My God, thank you."

Baker reclined in his chair, closed his eyes and took a deep breath. When he opened them again, he continued, "The vault was intact? All the procedures worked?"

"Exactly as you described, Mr. Baker," I replied.

"And the rest of the house?"

"Nearly destroyed."

Baker nodded. "I suspected as much." He paused. "Where is your ... associate? I remember there was another man when I hired you."

"An accident, Mr. Baker. He didn't make it out of the Crash Zone."

"I'm sorry to hear it," Baker said, though there was no sign of remorse in his voice. Instead, he caressed the top of the hard drive as if eager to access it. "Should his portion of the fee be remitted to any next of kin?" he asked mechanically.

"There's no one that I'm aware of."

"All the better for you, then." Baker uttered a bark of a laugh and waved toward the door. "Susan outside will take care of you."

Assuming I was dismissed, I started to leave the office. Baker stopped me with a word.

"Would you like to see?" he asked.

I turned to find that he had removed the hard drive from the case and was in the process of hooking it to the computer on his desk.

"I don't think that would be appropriate, Mr. Baker," I replied, though inside, my curiosity was piqued—rarely did clients offer this kind of disclosure.

"It's important to me to show someone else," he said. "To verify they're real."

I shrugged and made my way toward the other side of the desk. For one million dollars, the least I could do was indulge the man.

I stared at the screen, expecting to see the wireframe model of a new product or perhaps an outline of the company's ten-year plan. But Baker navigated past the encryption safeguards and opened a video file instead, and I was immediately annoyed that I had been sent into the Crash Zone and lost my partner to retrieve what was likely a bunch of unaired commercials—or worse, some pervert's porno stash, as Serge had suspected.

Instead, the video began with an attractive woman in a one-piece bathing suit, sunglasses and a large-brim hat sitting by an in-ground swimming pool. A little girl played in the water, laughing gleefully as she splashed and the sunlight caught the droplets like a handful of thrown diamonds. Manicured lawns spread away from the pool in all directions, except in the left corner of the frame, where a small house occupied the landscape.

"I imagine the place is a wreck now," Baker said, half to himself. Then, as if remembering that I was there, he added, "My wife and daughter. Both were...at home during the asteroid strike. This drive"—he patted the hard drive again—"contains all of our family photos and videos. It's the only copy I have." He laughed sardonically. "What kind of tech CEO doesn't backup his own data?"

The video continued shakily — the camera was clearly being held by hand — as the little girl got out of the pool and hugged her mother. The woman squirmed away from her daughter's wet body, then laughed and returned the embrace lovingly.

Baker stopped the video.

"Thank you," he said again, and then began to ignore me completely, browsing through the other files on the drive, making sure all the data was there.

This time, I knew I had been dismissed. I exited the office and went to see Susan, the secretary. We began some small talk as she processed the wire transfer, and a strange sensation began in my chest that had nothing to do with my new riches.

ଔ

Patrick Scalisi *is an emerging author from Connecticut whose short fiction has appeared in* The Willows, *ReadShort-Fiction.com and the Aurora Award-winning magazine* Neo-opsis, *among others. His work has also appeared in five printed anthologies, and his debut book* The Horse Thieves and Other Tales of the New West *was released in the summer of 2014.*

THE MEN THAT HAVE TRANSGRESSED

ADRIAN CHAMBERLIN

And they shall go forth, and look upon the carcasses of the men that have transgressed against me: for their worm shall not die, neither shall their fire be quenched; and they shall be an abhorring unto all flesh."

Isaiah, 66:24, King James Bible

The last prophet paused before the Lions' Gate as he considered the words of his ancient predecessor. It was strange to have thoughts of Gehenna and everlasting fire upon entering Jerusalem; the eastern side of the Holy City was untouched by the holocaust, and should have been the sole beacon of hope and eternal life in a land devastated by nuclear rage. So it would be, were it not for its newest inhabitants. To the outside world, the one the prophet had left behind, this sole surviving entrance to the ancient citadel no longer led to a Holy City; it was the entrance to Hell.

"*Flevit super illam,*" he muttered, his voice barely a whisper, ravaged by radioactive snow and the unquenchable thirst that followed his ill-advised consumption of it. *Flevit super illam*...Christ may indeed have wept over it, pondering the suffering that would befall Jerusalem. Would He do the same now?

The Mount of Olives was a wasteland; the trees twisted and gnarled clusters of wood, frozen in death under a sprinkling of snow, as grey as crematoria ash, screaming their last to the black shroud of cloud. The prophet's descent to the Holy City had been along a landscape as lifeless and desolate as the Jewish Cemeteries. He resisted a shudder at the memory of the devastated ancient tombs he had passed in the Kidron Valley, the pyramid cap of Zechariah's tomb and the bottle-shaped Pillar of Absalom blasted into tumbledown rubble. Jehoshaphat it was known as in the Old Testament—"Yahweh Judges". And maybe God indeed had judged the dead of this ancient mount, reneged on his promise to resurrect mankind and consigned them to the oblivion of their own unearthly fire.

No, the prophet told himself, gazing at the two carved lions either side of the Gate. *The Day of Judgement has yet to dawn.* Not that there would be much of a dawn; the sun had not penetrated the cloud cover of the Holy Land since the ash descended and the nuclear winter began. How many years was it now?

The lions stared blankly at him from their sixteenth-century prison, unable—or unwilling—to answer. Patches of grey snow smeared the crenulated wall, and yet the pale gold of the sandstone was unaffected by this. It seemed to shine with an inner luminescence, or perhaps that was the paint of the lions. He allowed his cracked lips to part in a broken-toothed grin. He had to admire the brazen spirit of these new inhabitants; the Transgressors no longer hid themselves, even boldly claimed ownership of the Holy City with their alteration of the stone cats. Just as they had altered their own forms.

The prophet raised his head and stared closer at the stylised carvings.

The claws were more pronounced, sharper; demonic talons. The tails were segmented, each surmounted by a dagger-like sting. Bat-like wings had been added, half-opened as if in preparation for flight; the talon surmounting each opened like a desert bloom, with fresh blades budding. Yet the facial features were the most disturbing. They were beautiful.

They were almost human. Of indeterminate age, and androgynous, their appearance transcended mere human conceptions of beauty. These were the faces of angels, upon the bodies of nightmare.

This was the paradox at the heart of the New Jerusalem. The monsters within looked to God.

And where is God now? Each of the sacred sites had been blasted, and only ruins remained. The Dome of the Rock still stood, but from the Mount of Olives the prophet had seen for himself the devastation wrought by the war. The dome was a shattered eggshell of a ruin – the gold leaf had melted and ran down the original copper work, staining the drum and arcade like the tears of God. Before his death, the Israeli Defence Force captain had told him how the Western Wall had been levelled by the aftershocks of the earthquake, the huge lower stones of the Herodian period tumbling under the rainfall of those of the early

Islamic times. The last piece of the Second Temple—now completely destroyed.

There would be no more lamentation. There was no more Wailing Wall.

He would see for himself what remained of the Church of the Holy Sepulchre, at the end of the Via Dolorosa, before heading to his final destination at Temple Mount. He did not expect much; if the Hebrew and Muslim God had failed to prevent the destruction of His followers' most sacred sites, what hope of succour for that of the Christian?

To walk the Via Dolorosa, to follow the Way of Sorrow, seemed a fitting way to discover the truth for himself. It did not matter that the pathway of Jesus, taken on His way to execution and sacrifice, owed more to tradition than historical fact—the route had changed several times over the centuries—what was important was the symbolic nature of the journey.

His worn boot heels echoed as he passed through the gateway. A small piece of metal trapped in the sole of his boot made a screeching sound on the pavement which was amplified by the stone gateway; the noise filled his ears. He froze and glanced over his shoulder, momentarily convinced the lions had come to life, scraping their talons on the stone that imprisoned them within the Lions' Gate.

Grey, gelid cloud filled the view. The Mount was no longer visible, and nothing stirred in the stone above him. Nevertheless, he trembled, and clutched the shoulder straps of his rucksack tighter before proceeding. What he carried could not be lost—or indeed, taken—lightly.

It must be given.

The lack of pedestrians—pilgrims and otherwise—on what would normally be a busy thoroughfare disturbed him, and he forced his weary legs to quicken their pace. He kept his eyes on the ground as he passed the strangely intact Madrasa el Omariyya, which stood on the site of the Roman fortress Antonia, where Pilate had condemned Christ.

The First Station.

Unlike the pilgrims of before, he did not stay for prayer or meditation. He felt the weight of millennia upon his shoulders, the death sentence as palpable as it must have been to the ears of the Nazarene and His followers all those years ago.

No sound echoed save the prophet's unsteady footfalls and the shard of metal in his boot, scraping the stone flagged road. There were few remains of the gaudy shops and stalls whose owners had once hawked tatty souvenirs to the pilgrims; commerce and life had disappeared, and the prophet could meditate in silence upon the significance of the Christian saviour's journey, walking to His death, alone, with only His burden for company.

With each step down the Via Dolorosa, the weight within his rucksack increased, pulling on his shoulders and forcing him to stoop. One of the shoulder straps kept loosening, and he had to pause to tighten it. Sharpened edges of the offering pressed into his back as, less than fifty yards later, he passed the Franciscan Monastery of the Flagellation. Like the Madrasa, it had not been touched by the devastation. He winced.

He was certain he could smell blood; feel it, dripping down his forehead. He raised his free hand and tentatively caressed the sores on his face, winced at the stabbing pain and smell of pus that accompanied the watery blood.

The kiss of the nuclear wasteland upon his face had given him the seeds to his own Crown of Thorns. Now, at the Second Station, they gave fruit. His vision blurred and he became light-headed.

Coincidence, nothing more. Weariness from lack of sustenance, skin eruptions from exposure to the radioactive slagheap of the Holy Land. That's all.

But it was more than two hundred yards before the junction with the El-Wad Road, and the Third Station, where Christ had fallen beneath the weight of the cross for the first time. The prophet no longer believed he would get so far.

His back felt sore, as though lashed with a whip. Beneath the weight of his own burden, he felt the nuclear winter air press into the holes of his ragged overcoat. He dared not look to see if the rucksack had finally succumbed to the intolerable pressures of the thing it had been forced to contain since making landfall at the ruins of Tel Aviv, so long ago.

Curtains of red mist narrowed his vision, and made the gold sandstone of the buildings flare scarlet as they pressed in on him. He stumbled onwards, anxious to pass through the archway that bridged the Via Dolorosa before the walls crushed him.

Shadows fluttered along the now-red stone; liquid-black against burning scarlet. Lizard-like creatures traversed the walls on silent, spidery limbs, mounting the roof of the central bay. A multitude of recessed eyes within wedge-shaped faces flared gold as they glared at him. They squatted on spindle-limbs that elongated, became a forest of twisted arachnid limbs that supported bloated, pulsating torsos that glowed with incandescence.

It rained fire. Hot flames scoured his upraised palms as he stared in terror at the creatures that lined the arch through which Pilate had presented Christ to the crowds.

"Ecce Homo," the creatures chorused, in a scratchy parody of a human choir. *"Ecce Homo!"*

Behold the man. The prophet turned, and the shoulder strap of his rucksack slipped loose. Its burden swung freely. His centre of gravity was upset, his balance lost, just as new arrivals shot from the darkened recesses of the arch. Grey, nozzle-like protuberances extended from their groins, swelling like aroused penises, ready to unleash their seed like their comrades had.

"Ecce Homo! Ecce Homo!"

He fell to the ground and his burden slammed into his side. Liquid fire coated the flagstones, turning the Way of the Cross into a new holocaust. His eyes took in the sky, and more of the creatures appeared, oozing from behind the dome of the Convent of the Sisters of Zion. The napalm-dealing appendage of one wrapped itself around the spire and the iron cross briefly glowed scarlet before melting into a thick globule of metallic lava.

He had a vision of the blasted Dome of the Rock with its molten gold-leaf. *The tears of God. Here, the sperm of Satan. "Their worm shall not die, neither shall their fire be quenched." Jerusalem has truly become Gehenna.*

The rags of his overcoat and trousers smouldered; his flesh shrieked. His own screams were inaudible over the triumphant cry of the beasts.

Triumph became terror. A rise in pitch, and a change in timbre, as the creatures shrieked in their own pain. Skeletal claws that dug into his flesh withdrew immediately, and he felt softer, wider hands scoop his burning body from the molten lava of the flagstones. Claws retracted and powerful digits extended, curled around his torso, as they bore him into the sky.

The fire behind him, and then below, and he felt cool air soothe his bloody, pus-stained brow; air from the beating of wings and the forward motion of the creature that carried him. He had a brief image of the beast's face before it pressed him into its furry chest. Golden fur, warm and thick. The coat of a lion soothed his brow and extinguished the last flames that burned his hair, while the face of an angel smiled at him.

ભ

He journeyed through a night brought on by unconsciousness, the wings of his angel beating softly, rhythmically. He had new visions: glimpses of the Church of the Holy Sepulchre, and the fate that had befallen it. There were no outward signs of destruction; the Rotunda and the Catholikon Dome were intact, but the crosses had been removed, replaced with something indefinable but disturbing. Serpentine, unearthly, and far from holy. The icon of the new monsters at the heart of Jerusalem.

He saw now the source of the creatures — not from behind the Ecce Homo arch, nor the Convent. That was merely the advance guard, now joined by hordes of the monsters from the Church of the Holy Sepulchre, swarming from the courtyard of the basilica and the Muristan to join the Via Dolorosa, like baby spiders released from their egg sac and hungry for new meat. He groaned in despair.

Christ's Tomb, defiled by the Transgressors. I did not foresee this.

Had the Vision been wrong? The monsters he had been sent to destroy, the lions with faces of angels — were they his saviours now?

He heard whispered voices talking above him. Apart from a faint trace of an Arabic accent, their tones were musical, chiming; the sound he expected angels to make.

These are no angels, he reminded himself. *They too are Transgressors — demons!*

"Would a demon save your life, human?"

His eyes snapped open. He saw a circular panorama of blue and white tiles — floral descriptions and Arabic inscriptions, breathtaking in their beauty. He counted seventeen columns, and he knew where he was.

The Dome of the Chain. The monsters had taken refuge in Temple Mount, the Haram esh-Sharif.

"Noble sanctuary" indeed.

Angels' faces moved into view, and the light from them seemed to illuminate his surroundings.

Rough paws applied dampened cloths to his forehead, an ointment that cooled and energised him. He felt strong enough to sit up.

His clothes were gone. The rags of the old Israeli Defence Force uniform, his overcoat, and his worn boots, had been replaced with a plain robe of red silk. The sores on his calves and feet were faded, healing. He saw discarded cloths soaked with blood and pus, smelling of exotic herbs, and guessed the beasts had ministered to the wounds all over his body.

"I don't know. Why did you save me?" His voice was clear; the strength and command of a former military tone had returned. His words echoed.

Two leonine creatures squatted before him. He took a sharp intake of breath at the sheer beauty of their faces, the brindled neck-fur halos. Their eyes were pure, liquid gold, filled with a light that seemed to come from Heaven itself, discordant to the demonic bat-like wings, folded and flat against their backs, the coiled and retracted scorpion tails, and the inch-thick talons that glistened like ebony on the thick red carpets.

"You are...American?" one ventured, in a voice that was neither male nor female. It rose and moved forward, its nostrils flaring as it inhaled his scent. The pupil-less eyes stared into him. It hissed, and the flowing gold darkened, clotted momentarily. Anger or disapproval, he wondered. "No, not American...Canadian."

"You are a long way from home." The one nearest him cocked its head quizzically. It too spoke in an androgynous voice, though there was something in the delivery that hinted at a greater age than its companions. Perhaps sadness, a trace of weariness. "Jerusalem has not received pilgrims since the Cleansing Fires. What brings you here?"

"A vision," he said slowly. "Of holy fire...and rebirth in the centre of Christ's tomb. Salvation for mankind. The Tribulation has passed. Now is the time for Rapture."

"A prophet, then. And you are the one chosen to deliver this to the world?" There was a mocking lilt in the beast's tone. "Of all the madness the Holy City inspires, 'Messiah Complex' is one we believed to have passed. What are your credentials, *prophet?*"

Motes of dust danced in the air above the creatures, turned to gold by the light from their eyes. He wondered if it was masonry dust or radioactive ashes. Perhaps grave dust, pounded human bone mixed from the shattered sepulchres of the Holy City. Despite the glory of his surroundings, the architecture of a city inspired by three faiths, this was a reminder that Jerusalem was now nothing more than a necropolis. A city fit only for death and monsters.

Ready for deliverance.

The first creature followed his gaze. "One tradition holds this to be the centre of the world. It is also said that a chain once hung from the roof, and whoever told a lie while holding it would be struck dead by lightning."

"We have no need for that," the second creature said. "There is no falsehood here. With the near extinction of the human race and the ascendancy of the ones your kin insultingly call Transgressors, lies have no place." It shifted, and extended a paw to the battered rucksack the prophet had borne into the Holy City. "Yet still you come, like the crusaders of old, determined to bring fire and sword to the new citizens of the Holy City."

The talon of its middle finger extended and swept horizontally. A slit appeared in the canvas, and the prophet's burden was revealed. Sadness filled the creature's voice. With its angelic tones, the effect was heartbreaking. "Your predecessors preached an old creed, one of destruction. One that still persists, has no need in a world turned to ash. And you call *us* monsters?"

The prophet's heart sank. He couldn't meet the creature's eyes. There was no anger or righteous fury in those golden orbs, just a calm, inhuman judgement. He stared at his feet. The sores had healed completely.

"You call us Transgressors, merely because we embraced the dark spirits that poured from the harrowed earth and accepted their gift of transformation. You are wrong, prophet. We have not transgressed the laws of God and Nature; we have *transcended* them.

"My companion is Al-Burak; it is she who flew you here." A faint smile. "A nocturnal journey through the skies, like the prophet Mohammed's Night Flight. My name is Ta'lab. Rise, and walk with me."

ଓ

Despite his thin robe, the prophet didn't feel cold. The healing ointments imbibed his body with a warmth, and a strength, he had not felt in…

How long has it been? Months, years? He didn't know. He only had vague memories of meeting the three-man team from what used to be the Israeli Defence Force in the ruins of Tel Aviv, and their jeep journey southeast before…*before what? What happened to them, and why was I walking, alone?*

The esplanade retained some of its glory, despite the holocaust. The cypress trees had long been blasted to ash, but the qanatirs remained, and through one the prophet had a clear view of the Gate of Mercy. The sixteenth-century material used to wall it up by the Muslims lay in crumbled fragments, and gave view to the desolation beyond. A paw rested on his shoulder. He stiffened, and was then aware of how strong his arm was; well-toned muscles ready for physical action. Military action.

What am I?

"It was foretold amongst one of your tribes that a Messiah would enter Jerusalem through this gate. It was one of the first structures to fall when the bombs fell. But has a Messiah come?"

The prophet turned. In the perpetual overcast and the ruins of the Temple Mount, Ta'lab looked diminished, its angelic glory dimmed. "We are the last of our kind, prophet."

The prophet stared at the broken shell of the Dome of the Rock. Its glory was as pale as Ta'lab's. Beyond, he saw the ruins of the Western Wall and the final destruction of Solomon's Temple.

"From the ruins of Gaza we came, an ancient and noble spirit unleashed by the nuclear fire giving us the form and name *manticore*, while a darker, more destructive spirit older than Christ was reborn in the church that bears His name. Its corruption combined with the Miracle of the Holy Fire, and gave birth to the creatures that attacked you."

"A different breed of Transgressor, then—but still monsters." *Like you*, he mentally added, and Ta'lab's eyes flashed in anger.

"We are *not* like they. They are an abomination, the physical manifestation of mankind's spiritual bankruptcy."

Now the prophet felt a chill run through his healed body, but it was not the cold of the nuclear winter—it was the cold of realisation.

"Did your companions not mention this to you?" There was an appraising look in Ta'lab's golden eyes as its voice resumed its angelic, melodic quality. "When they gave you the burden to lay upon Jerusalem? Did they not promise to accompany you into the city?"

"I...we drove here. But all I remember is walking..."

"Tell me of your Vision. Think hard, prophet. You will realise your God spoke to you after you arrived in the Holy Land, not before."

Tears stung the prophet's eyes. "Fire. That's all I can remember. Holy Fire, and the Voice of God. A commandment to purify the Holy City for the coming of the Messiah."

Ta'lab nodded slowly. "Fire. And did this fire consume your companions and your vehicle? A divine test of your resolve and purpose, rather than an exploded fuel tank from a poorly-maintained military vehicle, commandeered by a demobilized military unit that sees us as subhuman, wishes to wipe us out like they destroyed Gaza and its peoples?"

The prophet stared at Ta'lab through a curtain of tears. The angelic beauty was smeared, yet still radiant: the only pure thing he had experienced in Jerusalem.

Fire. Had not God spoken to him, commanded him to walk the Way of Sorrow before approaching the Dome of the Rock with His holy gift of cleansing? Had he not judged his companions as unworthy?

"No...you're wrong."

"Am I? Why were you summoned from Canada? There are no battles to be fought there, and a man of your military experience could better serve humanity on another theatre of conflict. With no more of your fellow men to fight and kill, it was inevitable that the next target would be 'monsters'. Free Jerusalem from the occupiers; make it pure and sanctified, and all will be well." Disgust tempered its lilting tone. "How many times has this story been told?

"Look there, prophet." Ta'lab pointed to a building just visible behind the outer ambulatory of the Dome of the Rock. It was one of the few buildings relatively unscarred by the apocalypse, but when he wiped his eyes, the prophet realised it had been subject to rebuilding. The Mamluk architecture was uneven, additions from other buildings clearly obvious—and clearly obvious that the two lion-creatures venerated this building more than any other in Jerusalem. "The Dome of Learning. It is where I and Al-Burak spend our days—and nights. *Learning*. There is such a wealth of knowledge, much of which was hidden from infidels' eyes. Indeed, any of your tribes would have difficulty understanding the lessons the ancient scrolls and parchments have to teach. We have been studying them for decades, and have an understanding of them you could never have. We understand the purpose of what you call God, and the division between man and monster."

The building looked forbidding to him. He didn't take solace in the creature's words; he took offence.

"So, a monster can understand the word of God, but not a man?" His words were snarled.

Ta'lab's body stiffened. Its folded wings twitched, its segmented tail trembled, and its talons glinted black before he regained control. The claws retracted.

"*Ecce Homo... Ecce Monstrum*. Man and monster are similar in many respects. They both misunderstand and misinterpret."

The prophet was emboldened. Righteousness replaced the self-doubt. And was it not a monster, one of the Transgressors, who had planted that seed of doubt within him?

"Show me," he said. Without waiting for a reply, he strode towards the reconstructed Madrasa, barely noticing the rubble and shale that cut his feet.

The darkness within was thick, tangible; the bookshelves and scripture holders were silhouettes, the secrets they held hidden in the dark. He sniffed, surprised to sense no trace of dust or ash. He smelled fresh ink, watercolour paints and paper.

It was useless to search for a candle or a match with which to light one; Ta'lab and its companion had made it clear in the Dome of the Chain that they were comfortable with the dark, that their golden eyes had the power to penetrate darkness, pierce it with their own illumination.

He heard heavy, furred footprints echo through the vestibule, a slow and measured approach from Ta'lab that signified the monster was in no hurry to show—or deny—the prophet the secrets it had found.

Golden globes spilled angelic light upon the interior, and the prophet gasped at the translation of the literary treasure before him.

"We do not know when your race will rebuild itself sufficiently to embrace civilisation once more," Ta'lab said softly. "Future generations may not understand the languages you and I speak now. Pictures, symbols, are our preferred method of presenting the secrets of God...and Man."

The work in progress was on a low bench before him, the canvas stretched on a frame. The prophet stared in bewilderment, then horror, and finally anger at the beautifully painted images.

"The tears of God, the sperm of Satan...there is no difference," Ta'lab said with an expressive paw, its talons carefully retracted. "Merely cosmic energy, imbibed with holiness or evil by those who use it."

The creatures that infested the Church of the Holy Sepulchre, the lion-beasts that had taken control of Jerusalem, and the source of their mystery and power—and ultimately, their destiny—lay before the prophet, in a form that even the simplest, most backwards human child would understand.

It went beyond blasphemy. It was a negation of the miracle of Man, a denigration of his achievements and his relationship to God. The chosen ones who would lead all races out of the darkness into a new light of civilisation had the bodies of lions, the tails of scorpions, the wings and talons of demons, and the faces of angels.

False angels. This is abomination. He moved away from the canvas, his way lit by the searching eyes of Ta'lab.

"We have to feed," the monster said. "But our appetites are not as voracious as the things unleashed by the war between the Hebrews and the Palestinians. Is the firstborn son of each couple really too much to ask? Did Yahweh not command Abraham to give unto Him his son Isaac, on this very place?"

The prophet paled. On shaking legs, he turned and ran into the esplanade. The golden crown of the Dome of the Rock was tarnished forever more; the same gold as that which filled the creatures' eyes. A shrine to an abandoned sacrifice, a test of one man's faith in his God. Now it would be a slaughterhouse for future generations of humanity.

"We would not rule over you, prophet." Ta'lab's voice thundered through the Noble Sanctuary, the lullaby tones now a crashing crescendo of strings and bass. "We would guide you, show you how to regrow, to heal the scorched earth and reap bounty from desolation. We will help your race achieve its true, sacred potential, to understand and harness the secret powers of the universe as we have done. We would not even expect you to worship us. Merely feed us when we require."

Beating wings cracked the black sky above. He looked up, froze in horror at the sight of Ta'lab's companion, ascending from the shattered dome, with the prophet's burden clutched to its chest. There was a look of such serenity, such triumph in Al-Burak's face that the prophet wished he was back in the Via Dolorosa, facing death from those napalm-wielding demons.

Al-Burak alighted before him. Its wings folded, and its segmented tail withdrew. Only shreds of the canvas rucksack remained. The dull grey cylinder with its radiation warning labels, its buttons and dials, was clearly visible, its purpose obvious. Al-Burak knelt and held the bomb out to the prophet. There was no mockery in its posture.

"It is choice that makes you human," Ta'lab whispered in his ear. "We are not monsters. We do not decree, or demand. The decision is yours."

The prophet held the device in trembling hands and pressed it into his chest. The cold steel penetrated his thin robe, chilled him to the very core of his being. The burden he had carried into the Holy City felt even heavier than before.

"Turn Jerusalem into a true necropolis, banish all hope of a return to civilisation, and allow a new breed of monster to flourish. Fulfil your 'holy crusade'. Or trust in us." Al-Burak rose to its feet. Ta'lab also withdrew, and the prophet found himself standing, alone, on the site sacred to three faiths, with the power to destroy it, and a decision he could not make.

The dials and switches felt like talons. They cut into his fingers. He sank to his knees, tears filling his eyes, sobs racking his body.

"Ecce Homo," he murmured, and waited for God to guide him.

෨

Adrian Chamberlin *is a British writer of dark fiction. He has had short stories published in British, American, Canadian, and Australasian anthologies, and his first novel* The Caretakers *was published by Dark Continents Publishing in 2011 to considerable critical acclaim. He has also edited for* Hersham Horror Books, Wicked East Press, *and the* Lovecraft eZine. *His most recent work 'Serpents of Albion' appeared in Innsmouth Free Press's* **Sword and Mythos** *anthology. Further details can be found on his website* www.archivesofpain.com

SAND CASTLES

MATTHEW SPENCE

He never liked going out into the Desert alone. Nobody did, but his was a special case. They need him out here, because there weren't many around these days with his extraction skills. So, every six months, he, Doctor Singh, was sent out. In earlier times he might have been flattered that they still thought so highly of his skills, but now Singh knew that he was chosen simply because nobody else wanted to go. Those that were old enough didn't want to remember the Swarms and what they'd done, even though the evidence was around elsewhere. The Ghost Towns, which still had the best samples, were the most obvious reminders, but they could be forgotten as long as they were avoided long enough. It wasn't so simple for Singh and those like him.

"We need reports," the Provisional Council always told him. "Everyone gets their turn. You're a thorough specialist." The woman who delivered the news this time was older, someone who'd been a child when the Swarm happened. Her skin still bore the marks of secondary infection; white scars that lined her face and arms.

"I understand." The Zones were still officially under quarantine, after all, even though the government that had enforced that quarantine, along with the various agencies that were supposed to keep track of the original outbreak, no longer existed. But the settlements that had grown up out of refugee camps were still there, and they needed people like him.

"Be careful," the woman said, as he left the Council's tent.

Singh nodded. "Every sample log shows they've been inert for years. I'll be fine." He left, taking his small kit with him, climbing into his waiting rover, feeling the scale of the world outside the Settlement underneath the perpetually dusky sky, still littered with Swarm debris, as he drove off.

The desert gave no sign of infection itself. There was life out here; and some signs of renewal. The rover's tracking systems showed a drone, from one of the larger settlements, somewhere overhead. Looking at the sky, Singh could see its trail in the distance. There was competition between other settlements for samples, which his own smaller community tried to stay out of. Singh had heard of other samplers being paid as "bounty hunters" for their work, but Singh's work was more or less steady, and he got regular ration credits for it. He'd never encountered the so-called hunters, although Singh knew they were out here. The Council knew as well—it was scouts and still-functioning satellites that had found this particular town, before the other settlements had. There was value in the knowledge that the samples could provide, both good and bad.

As always, the first thing Singh noticed as he approached the town in his Swarm-proofed rover was how normal everything still looked, especially from a distance. The closer he got, however, the more Singh saw the truth. The buildings, while still standing, looked as they had been sculpted out of the surrounding sand. And the people, still frozen where they'd been caught, their faces showing normal emotions, with no idea of what had happened to them, caught in time as well.

Singh told the rover to stop and wait for him. He couldn't help glance down as he took his sampler with him and made his rounds. He knew that the Statues technically weren't alive, but Singh couldn't help feel that they were still looking at him, perhaps wondering if this was going to be the day that they were finally released. *Well, here I am,* Singh thought as he approached one woman's figure. *Back to make my rounds, as always. Don't worry; I'll just take my samples and then be on my way...*

Singh liked to think of them as "his" patients. They were all compete strangers—people caught in ordinary acts, bound together by the same fate, but to Singh they had become as familiar to him as his own neighbors and family might have been. Singh went to each of them, carefully drawing stagnant nano samples from their frozen bloodstreams. There was a ten-year-old girl, caught in mid-skip, an elderly man who as now reading the same page of a magazine forever, and the woman, whose sample came next. She had the expression of someone who'd been distracted by something that she couldn't understand; her eyes were fixed in a puzzled stare. One of the first targets, Singh thought. You saw it coming...but didn't even know what it was, did you?

Their bodies were impervious to the elements, as the nanos, before their redundancies failed, had been designed to do. Their skin was ash-white, turned into dead crystallized cells by the infection. The naos had been ruthlessly efficient in that regard, cannibalizing the cells for oxygen and their bodies for water for fuel. The Swarm itself had been programmed for a short lifespan-everyone agreed on that much. But it had taken a generation of victims before stopping, leaving them behind as reminders, as ghosts, like the Ghost Towns they still inhabited.

Singh finished with the first group, the one that was used as a control group by the researchers back in the Clean Zone. The ones who had been caught indoors were next. Singh always felt like he was invading their privacy the most, because they'd been frozen in personal, intimate acts. "I'm sorry about this," he said to the couple he found in bed. At least he didn't feel like they were looking at him-their attention was focused on each other. Maybe it still was.

"I know I've said this before," Singh said as he took one more sample, this time from a young woman caught in the act of talking on an antiquated smart phone. Who had she been talking to, he wondered? Was it a friend, a parent, a lover? Was that person still alive, or also frozen, along with her? "I wish I could make you understand what happened to you," Singh continued. "I wish I could say who was responsible, and what we've done to keep it from happening again. I'd like to tell you that you have been able to help others, because you have. I just wish there was some way I could tell all of you that."

There no response, of course. Sometimes, Singh thought he could almost see one in their eyes...but that was just an illusion. There were those who said they were the lucky ones, the ones who'd been caught first. Singh had seen Swarm victims, partially infected, their will and sanity taken from them. They were effectively immortal, a by-product of the Swarm, perhaps what it had originally been intended for. There had been experiments with life extension, back then. There were all sorts of theories, but for Singh, the only thing that mattered now were the results — and they were always the same.

The sun was beginning to set as Singh took his last sample. "Okay, that's about it," he told his last "Patient." He looked at the readings before putting the sampler back into his carrying case. One hundred percent infection rate, it read. No change in predicted behaviors. No change in cellular activity.

I don't know why I always talk to them, Singh thought as he climbed back inside the rover. It was getting darker. Ghost Towns always looked different at night, like they were still alive. Most other people had superstitions about that, staying away from the towns as if they were haunted. *They're still statues*, Singh reminded himself as he drove off. They're not ghosts or people who are simply asleep. They only thing haunting these towns are memories.

Singh took one last look around as he drove away, leaving a trail of dust as he went. Soon the town was empty and silent again.

Empty, except for its memories...

Singh saw the other rover as he left. It was parked about a mile away, its driver, face hidden behind a biohazard mask. The driver was watching as Singh drove past. A hunter, Singh thought, noticing the rover's heavy armor plating. It was close to nightfall; the other rover's lights were already on, and Singh could see that the car had an infra-red tracking system-and a gun turret. Not a legitimate hunter, then-a scavenger.

Singh's own rover wasn't armored, but it did have defenses. He'd never thought he'd have to use them, but Singh released a flood of micro-missiles as the other rover came, its engine hissing like a snake. The missiles were percussion types, designed to stun an enemy with overhead airbursts. The Council understood the need for its samplers to protect themselves, but preferred "civilized" means.

And it worked. The other rover, for its hissing and heavy armor, was stalled, its systems fried by a single electromagnetic pulse fired from the lead missile's warhead. The others made popping sounds over the driver's head as he (or she) tried to shield themselves, giving Singh time to get away.

The woman was waiting for Singh in the tent when he returned, and read his attached report file. "I'll communicate this to the other settlements," she said. "If somebody is paying scavengers for sample bounties, they'll want to know. Were there any other problems?"

Singh shook his head. "The town was the same. They were all just statues."

The woman nodded thoughtfully. "But they weren't always that way, were they? We've seen them, caught in their last acts, so ordinary to them. But not to us."

No, Singh thought. Never to us.

 catch

Matthew Spence *was born in Cleveland, Ohio and currently lives in Parkersburg, West Virginia. His work has appeared in* The Fifth Dimension, The Martian Wave, *and* SQ Mag.

THE HONEYSUCKLE SNOW

GREGORY L. NORRIS

It was impossible to not think of ghosts on that day as the convoy moved east, and the snow fell on sheets of diaphanous white mist. At points along the stretch of corridor, the trees grew close enough to form a living wall, a barrier through which only apparitions seemed capable of navigating.

In a town called Roth's Arbor, according to a fading sign barely visible through the press of evergreens, a marker likely to be swallowed whole a year from this winter date—not that names of towns or the Gregorian Calendar mattered anymore—Jonas saw the first worrying image: a red 'D' painted across the mottled white exterior of an old farmhouse. The house sat at an angle at odds with its foundation and leaned forward, as though its spine had shattered in the violent upheaval that had blasted it free of its joists. The face of the house frowned. The glass of its front windows was shattered, and Jonas made the terrible connection of eyes frozen open, burst capillaries in the shape of the splinters.

Jonas didn't realize he was staring, or that his mind had drifted—a potentially dangerous mistake along any stretch of the corridor but especially this section of the route, which led through the heart of Ground Zero. A fist to the shoulder jarred him out of the daze. Sommerkamp, no surprise there despite the unwelcome shock of the punch.

"Stop gawking—it's not polite," the other man said, certain syllables whistled through gaps in teeth and a filter of rangy beard. "You might catch one of them undressing."

"More likely undressing some poor soul of his or her hide," said Koogan, the group supervisor, who had all of his teeth; white ones that lent him a rabid look when he grinned, though they'd all gone wild to an extent. "You don't want to see one of them in the flesh, trust me, but you're gonna see lots of proof that they were here. Plenty more, after we come down from the mountains."

Jonas shook himself out of the sudden chill the air around him had taken.

"We go close, real close, past their territory."

Koogan grabbed Jonas's shoulders. A playful gesture, but Jonas resented the contact and walked two paces away, right up to the nearest transport wagon. The musky smell of the horses filled his next shallow sip of air.

Better than what's coming off Koogan and Sommerkamp, he thought.

Somehow, the secret insult broke the spell, and he was able to think again. Jonas adjusted the strap of his rifle, which had likely belonged to a soldier before the big collapse, and took up his position. The order to resume their press forward came down the line, from Alpha Company to Tango. The twenty units and their precious cargo of salt marched on; eventually, they passed through what remained of a tiny former town known as Roth's Arbor for another, also overgrown, also silent, its houses broken and listing askew by the forces that had on that unforgettable date clawed their way up from the unknown depths of the underworld.

ᛒ

Jonas felt the miles in his bones, deep in his marrow. At another point far behind them now, he had stopped to remove what he thought was a pebble or shard of wood in his right boot and had instead discovered the irritation was his own skin, rubbed off in abundance enough to have calcified into a chunk. Two of his toes routinely bled around the nails. There were days when his feet fell asleep and tingled with pins and needles, only they weren't kicked up on a mattress at an awkward angle but still in motion.

Jonas de Roek was twenty-four going on a hundred, according to the aches.

The route took a sharp turn around the base of a rise that was more hill than actual mountain. Still, gravity attempted to paralyze him. Then he caught sight of the first sign of former human civilization in what he was sure was a full continent's distance. Four miles, maybe, Jonas's inner voice corrected. Given conditions, they were lucky to have gotten four miles closer to the East Coast, where he hoped they would be safe.

More houses, each marked with the telltale stamp, some with several. Among them was a sad, sagging bungalow whose front porch was littered with leaves and shards of broken crockery before showing off an extensive sleeve of tattoos in spray paint down one side, proof of convoys past.

Koogan counted the red tags. Seventeen. He fished a can of spray paint out of his rucksack and added one more 'D.'

"He's brave," said Sommerkamp.

"Just doing his duty," Jonas fired back. "What happened here was a long time ago."

Ten years, give or take. Still, Jonas couldn't shake the terrible sensation that someone other than the militia or civilians gathered around the salt wagons was watching.

Only his imagination, Jonas told himself. This place was dead, and all it took was a glance to the left or the right, at one fractured house or another, to believe as much.

Snow fell. The convoy moved on.

ᚙ

The route dipped. A jagged chunk had been bitten out of the asphalt, only the damage owed to the river salivating over its banks and not the nightmares that had tunneled up and through the planet's surface. Fresh white drifted past on a restless wind. Jonas wondered if the snow had ever taken a break. Maybe, they were in the clutches of a new ice age. Perhaps the monstrous abominations living deep below the ground among sulfur and brimstone had, in leaving the center of the Earth, cooled it. Surely, they'd left behind vast tunnels. Nature hates a vacuum and rushes in to fill it, the voice of a former schoolteacher blathered in his thoughts. Images of glaciers and clacking, segmented limbs invaded his mind's eye.

Jonas's right foot cracked through a scree of rock, ice, and powder. He recovered before his ankle twisted, or worse. The edge of the pavement vanished, and the collapsed section of road immediately before him reminded Jonas of the hazards. He moved back into tight formation, close to Sommerkamp. Too close.

"You up for a skinny dip, guy?" the other man said.

Sommerkamp nudged him with an elbow.

"Stop it," Jonas said.

When Sommerkamp didn't heed the warning, Jonas shouted louder. Louder than he'd planned. Loud enough to carry up, up, past the surrounding stands of hemlock and skeletal paper-white birch trees, over the ruined steeple of a former country church, now just one more secret road sign covered in red graffiti. Past the canyon of snow-choked mountains, broadcast into the sky itself.

Boots ahead of him plodded to a halt, and faces turned. The pins and needles infecting Jonas from the calves down jumped up his legs and consumed the deepest parts of his body, freezing his core. Eyes focused upon him from every direction. Human eyes. Dog and horse, too. Worse, eyes that didn't blink and blazed red, in clusters of sixes and eights, somewhere out there in the new night, he was sure of it.

ः

They stopped to rest and eat along the river. The convoy was low on food, even lower on salt, and it was the latter that threatened to make his meal reappear soon after Jonas choked down the meager rations. The late supper had consisted of something gamy caught in the woods miles behind them and salted for preservation. And also for protection. While the company ate, the decision was made to make camp for the night. The road—what was left of it—was too perilous to attempt in the dark.

"You know what that means," said Koogan, his words spoken for all of Tango.

Sommerkamp started to complain. "But—"

"Grab a shovel and do your job, or I'll find something worse for you."

That was the end of the argument. Jonas marched into the line. Bodies formed a circle around the closest of the wagons, picked up shovels, and laid out a barrier of salt. All of the companies linked up, connecting the barrier around the convoy.

"Next stiff rain'll just wash it all away, into the river," Sommerkamp moaned after the salt circle was laid.

Washed away. Jonas ignored the sinking emotion in the deepest pit of his stomach and huddled in close to the new fire, which did little to dispel the early night's clutches. The salt on the game meat and the starchy hunk of bread in his guts sat foul over his tongue, now swollen from the meal and an imperfect fit in his mouth. *The people in the convoy had been salted like the ground around them*, he thought with a humorless chuckle.

Unlike food rations, safety, and salt, water was in abundance, in the snow, the river. Water, water, everywhere.

A chill worked its way past the layers of his clothes, around the wool scarf that stunk of neck sweat, and to the sensitive patch at his nape. Jonas fought it, failed. The chill tumbled down his spine. A single callous star mocked him through a break in the snow clouds. He needed to relieve himself. His mouth ached for fresh water. The fast-moving laughter of the river worsened his discomfort.

He approached Koogan. "Sir, I'll be right back."

"Take Sommerkamp with you."

"Also need to water the flowers."

"I don't care. Nobody strays."

Jonas nodded. Sighing through his nostrils, he found the other man from Tango Company jabbering with a handsome woman from either Sierra or Romeo he no doubt was interested in, at least for that night.

"That's what happened back in Muncie, I swear!" Sommerkamp said.

The woman batted his arm.

"Yo," Jonas said.

Sommerkamp and the woman gazed up. The fire lent a sharp, red glint to their eyes. "Hey, Koogan says..." he started, stopped. "Never mind."

Jonas turned and walked away from the two temporary lovebirds and the fire. The heat waned at his back. Salt crunched under the worn treads of his winter boots. The road and river loomed beyond the protective barrier, yards distant, too tempting a destination to ignore despite the danger of a single step.

He shifted the assault rifle's strap and marched over the salt. The dark landscape beyond was a dead realm, he sold himself. What happened here was over a decade ago. Days before the collapse, the world he knew as a kid was still intact, with cartoons and video games and grocery stores and stadium rock played at baseball games. A kingdom of men, believing themselves rulers of the earth, of Hell and Heaven. And then...

Jonas remembered how the ground shook that morning, the crash of plates and glasses as cabinets vomited out their contents onto the floor, and the flash of a nightmare image that couldn't be real: an oily-gray, segmented claw, colossal in scope, waving out of the middle of the ruined ranch house next door. All else after that was madness.

The horrors had moved inland, away from the coastlines. This was dead space now, a vast graveyard stretching hundreds of miles in all directions.

The river spilled past the destroyed road, liquid blackness reflecting the campfire. Jonas's boots found purchase on the rocks and chunks of asphalt. He hunched beside the water, worked off his right glove, scooped a handful to his lips, and sipped. The water was cold and free of the gritty quality of the swill in his canteen. He thought of cold root beer floats and summer lemonade, the water bubbler in grade school and frosty ginger ale—miracles long gone everywhere save for in his memories. Crisp mountain water, it tasted better than anything his body had known since the end of that other world.

Another sense triggered, and Jonas froze. The fragrance of flowers drifted among the snowflakes, subtle at first, but growing between sips of breath. The memory jumped out of his head and into the present. When the houses shook and the world turned upside down, he'd smelled exotic flowers, too. Like honeysuckle. *Them.*

Jonas willed his paralysis to break. He stood quickly. Pain raced up from his ankles. He ignored the jolts, reached for the rifle, and readied to fire.

The water streamed onward, objective in its purpose. Snow fell in wind-stirred eddies, equally neutral. The lone, uncaring star overhead winked out, eclipsed by the clouds. The fire's warmth and the safety of the salt circle looked miles away, not a distance of yards.

Jonas opened his mouth, intending to shout the alert. The too-sweet smell of flowers clotted atop his taste buds. Then the world phased out of focus, and the strength in his legs evaporated. Jonas fell. The drop to the earth seemed more like spiraling down, down into a bottomless chasm.

C3

The strange taste lingered on his tongue. Jonas opened his eyes, only to close them again against the glare of what he assumed was that old stranger, the sun. The light warmed his flesh. Jonas sucked in a breath, suddenly aware he'd held the last one in long enough that his lungs burned. On exhale, his eyes adjusted.

He woke in a strange bedroom, according to the antique brass fourpost with the porcelain finials, the alphabet sampler in the oblong, blue frame, and the old dresser with the beveled oval mirror suspended between carved wooden supports. Superhero stickers from a long lost era tattooed the mirror's circumference. Gossamer white curtains floated in the gentle breeze at two windows. Sunlight poured into the room, the air perfumed with flowers.

Jonas pinched his eyes and exhaled through his nostrils. "What the fuck?"

"You're awake," asked a voice. A woman's, sweet like honeysuckle.

Jonas glanced toward the bedroom door. She was his age, he guessed in the short time he drank in details: porcelain skin, blue eyes, freckles. Oh, how that last part triggered secret thoughts. While imagining how wonderful it would be to play connect-the-dots, he realized he'd gotten erect. Luckily, the bedclothes hid his guilt.

He shifted, intending to cover up better. Pain raced up his leg, driving the last of the fever-sleep away. Jonas bit back a swear. Freckles hurried over to him and placed one hand on his torso, the other on his upper leg.

"Don't move. The bones haven't had time to knit properly."

Jonas blinked the tears from his eyes, sending a thick pair sliding down his cheeks. "Knit?"

"You don't remember?"

The pain subsided enough that Jonas could think. "I remember Roth's Arbor, and the dead town after that. We were in Vermont, I think. Camped near Ground Zero. There was a river."

She laughed, but there was no humor in the sound. "That was months ago. You're at the ocean now — Hollings Head-by-the-Sea."

Jonas processed the information, eyes wide, mouth open, too. "Months? Why don't I remember any of that?"

"You suffered tragic and terrible things in Vermont. Maybe your mind closed itself off. No worries, though. Relax, you're safe now."

She patted his thigh. The caress sent electric pinpricks racing through Jonas's blood. All points on his flesh connected through the growing stiffness between his legs. She smiled, and his guilt worsened. Freckles looked an awful lot like a girl from a time and place whose details weren't so quickly forthcoming. Sierra Company, maybe, somewhere between the Midwest and the mountains.

"What's your name?" he asked.

Freckles smiled wider. "You know my name."

Jonas imagined the dopey, open-mouth look on his face.

"I'll be right back. Time to test your blood."

Jonas shrugged.

The beautiful stranger who looked familiar narrowed her eyes. "You don't remember that part, either? We're testing your blood regularly because of what happened back there, before we reached the ocean. When you got bitten."

Jonas broke focus with the woman's eyes — brown, flecked with gold — and inched his gaze down to his leg, which throbbed with renewed vengeance. The woman left the room. Outside, the background crash of waves grew softer, more melodious. Nature's lullaby.

Bitten. The ocean.

Jonas's eyelids grew heavy. Right before they dropped, plunging him into darkness, an image formed of a room superimposed over the one he presently inhabited. The other room was steeped in shadows and lacked comfort and warmth, the view outside one of winter wilderness glimpsed through shattered windows.

And then Jonas blanked out again.

ოჳ

Giant, hideous horrors, with clacking claws and carapaces covered in spikes, fins, swirls—patterns that left the unlucky witness with thoughts of runes cast by dark sorcerers. Runic exoskeletons. Those patterns got into your head, did things to the mind, screwed with vision; melted gray matter. It wasn't enough that the nightmares tunneling up from the depths, from *Hell*, blasted through houses, shopping malls, churches, and cities; one drop into those runic swirls, and the unlucky victim's skull was likely to blow apart, too.

"Evil fuckers," Jonas said.

Freckles withdrew the needle and carefully capped it. "What?"

"Those disgusting, dirty abominations."

She fixed him with a look, and ice slithered through his veins.

"Evil?" she said, the lone word sounding like an accusation. "They're many things. Destructive. Different. But I'd hardly call them evil."

Jonas shifted on the bed. Outside, waves crashed, heard but not seen. "You taken a good look at the world lately? Everything just about gone, given up, except for people lucky enough to make it to the coast or a salt lake. It's all blown up and busted, because of them. I call that evil."

She held the needle filled with his blood, and she no longer resembled the girl whose name he couldn't recall, source of so many past erections. "Who started this, after all?"

Started, he thought, and almost commented. But then Jonas decided better about it and held his tongue, because she no longer inspired his lust; he sensed she barely held her rage under control behind the façade of an icy smile.

"Who drilled the crust for geothermal energy, oil, *rocks*? Who *fracked* the strata, detonated underground nuclear bombs? They were here first, you know. They were down there for a long time, sleeping, and then we woke them up."

"Tell me how you really feel."

Her grin dropped. "I have a better perspective."

"Your name?"

"I told you."

Jonas choked down a dry swallow. He couldn't remember the last time he ate, but his stomach reminded him with its emptiness. A taste of gamy venison, heavily salted. The dryness in his throat wasn't from thirst but salt. Cold fear tickled him unpleasantly behind the testicles.

The words jumped out of his mind and past his lips before he could censor them. "Something that begins with 'D'?"

Her eyes locked with his, and in their depths, beyond the golden flecks, were mysteries and scary truths that paralyzed Jonas to the bed. He was aware of the room and the vague imagery of the ocean beyond wind-stirred curtains, though everything had flattened down to two dimensions. If he blinked, he was certain the details would dissolve between shutter clicks, because everything was window dressing. Nothing was real, except for him and her.

She lifted the syringe, red with his blood, examined it, and then him, and her beauty degraded enough for a fraction of a second that he saw the swirls and spells etched into her skin, those beguiling runes. The fragrance of honeysuckle grew stronger in his next shallow breath. He fell deeper into the incantation; Jonas's eyes again grew heavy.

D…

He returned to the river. In Vermont. The fractured road, undermined by the river. Under the road…

Something had been hiding under the road!

An explosion of sound dragged Jonas out of the fog. Lightning crackled again, and thunder followed. It sounded close, too close. Enough that he knew it wasn't the weather.

Gunfire, he thought.

He sat upright but was driven back down by the excruciating pain in his ankle. The agony cracked windows and walls, and drove the world apart, replacing it with a wash of angry red color. The red burned down, leaving a different room lit by the dying glow of the gray day beyond the shattered window glass.

"Over here! It's over here!"

More reports from gunshots, and shouts. Then hands seized hold of him. The world spun upside down, and vertigo punched Jonas in the guts. The sensation sent bile up his throat. Vomit painted his tongue. He tried to kick as agony overwhelmed him.

"Calm the hell down, dude," Sommerkamp said. "I got you. You're safe."

Before losing consciousness, Jonas absorbed the dark woods racing past, more explosions, and the snow surrounding them, which really hadn't melted and might never end.

☙

The pain was exquisite but helped Jonas to focus.

"You won't be able to walk on it. Not for a while, anyway," Koogan said.

Jonas could tell by the man's expression — and his own misery — that he might never walk on that leg again.

The flesh below the knee was a destroyed, discolored stretch of bite marks and sutures. An invisible fist punched Jonas in the guts. Koogan covered his leg with the blanket and set a hand on his shoulder, which anchored him back to the wagon and stopped him from falling down into the underworld contained within his imagination.

"At least you don't have to worry about walking for the foreseeable future," said Koogan.

"Yeah, there's that."

"Hey, you owe Sommerkamp. He went in there without hesitation, threw you over his shoulder, and got you out mostly in one piece. You'd think he actually liked you or something."

The joke got no more than a sigh.

"And her? That thing?"

Jonas leaned on the supervisor's shoulder. Sommerkamp moved toward the lump beneath the tarp laid out on one of the salt wagons, his rifle raised and at the ready just in case.

"Hold onto your breakfast," the other man said. "It ain't pretty."

It wasn't.

"Some kind of hybrid, we think," said Koogan.

Jonas turned his head away and focused instead on the patch of snowy forest and fractured road visible to the east. The creature's carapace and vague human features lingered clearly in his mind's eyes for long seconds after.

A hybrid, human and D. The conclusion posed more questions than it answered, and deepened Jonas's revulsion. Hybridization meant reproduction. An invisible fist punched him in the guts.

Sommerkamp said, "We found your girlfriend gnawing on you. Fucking cannibals."

Jonas shook his head. "No, she—it—was taking samples of my blood."

"So she's a vampire as well as a demon?"

Jonas again focused on the hideous corpse. His gaze drifted to the salt, and the truth sank in. "I think they're trying to adapt to all the extra salt in our blood. Adapting. God help us."

It was impossible to not think of ghosts that next day, as the convoy moved east, and the snow fell on sheets of diaphanous white mist.

CS

Gregory L. Norris *is a professional writer with work published in numerous national magazines and short fiction anthologies. He has also worked as a TV and film writer, and is the author of several novels and short story collections. The inspiration for "The Honeysuckle Snow" came during a long winter drive through rural Vermont while en route to a writing retreat. Follow Norris's literary adventures at* www.gregorylnorris.blogspot.com.

ADVANCED OCEANOGRAPHY

GARY EVERY

1

A shipment of Nike shoes spills overboard into the ocean, riding swift current streams, traversing the expansive Pacific. The traveling tennis shoes wash upon the western shore of North America, never to be worn again, mated pairs tragically separated by their castaway adventures. Some tennis shoes land as far south as Santa Barbara, California while others ride the frigid surf as far north as Ketchikan, Alaska.

An oceanographer takes careful notes measuring each and every voyage. Most of the shoes touch the blessed sanctuary of sandy shore on the beaches of Oregon, not far from the Nike factory as if they are spawning salmon returning home. This wet and soggy footwear journeys across the biggest ocean in the world, thousands and thousands of miles, before returning home without leaving behind a single footprint, without a single soul taking up space between the laces.

2

Two years later another cargo ship loses three merchandise containers overboard. Tossed among the waves, are tens of thousands of bathtub toys. An entire flotilla of rubber ducks is set free to roam the waves for all eternity. Thousands and thousands of yellow plastic ducks float atop the sea, a sight to see more grand than any Spanish Armada. The ducks ride from Indonesia past Japan and then come ashore at the beaches of Sitka, Alaska like soldiers storming Normandy. At least most of the rubber ducks come ashore at Alaska, some rubber ducks ride the surf and waves, pass by the land in disdain choosing an aquatic adventure and take another lap around the world. Ocean currents spin in long elliptical circles and every eight years the rubber ducks reach Sitka, Alaska, like swallows returning to Capistrano, the rubber ducks migrate back to Sitka and a few of them land and a few choose to circle around the earth one more time.

This journey circumnavigating the globe takes eight years like clockwork. In speedboat, sailboat, motorboat, row boat, tug boat, and trash barge, the oceanographer follows the rubber ducks, measuring, taking notes, and drawing maps. The oceanographer makes one major discovery and then slowly goes mad. He was a mad scientist don't you know. He realizes the intervals in the length of the cycles of the global ocean currents, one, three, five, seven and eight years, form a perfect major chord. The rhythms of the waters of the world measure their journey from beginning to end by forming a perfect major chord and singing in harmony.

3

On the bottom of the sea sediment in every ocean on the planet is a layer of plastic trash, bags, tools, toys, stoppers, snappers, and buttons. A thin layer of plastic garbage debris soils the bottom of the sea like industrial diarrhea. In some places the layer of plastic trash is ten times deeper than the plankton upon which every sea creature eventually feeds. Someday future archeologists will write textbooks declaring "In the era of the Plastic People these stupid morons nearly killed off our planet by poisoning the oceans."

The oceanographer was pondering and thinking about the best way to stop the insanity of this polluting horde of humanity. In every ocean, every sea he had found little toy soldiers bobbing in the waves. He had found little plastic men in the deepest of waters and shallowest tide pools. The mad scientist collects the little army men, usually green but sometimes red, blue, yellow, white, or gray, whom he gathers up, washes and gives a home. The oceanographer's merman military is growing stronger every day, filled with castaway toys and abandoned forgotten plastic soldiers. This scientist has gone quite mad—the way he laughs it makes me afraid. The other day this ostracized oceanographer walked into the room with a long flowing beard and carrying a trident—demanding that I call him Poseidon.

I started building an ark, just call it a hunch.

My wife thinks I am nuts.

4

An army of a trillion tiny little plastic men gather along the beaches of China. Tiny toy soldiers stand on each other's shoulders one after another after another after another. Tiny little plastic warriors stack themselves in giant pyramids, towering hundreds of feet above the beach. The mad oceanographer, long beard flowing in the breeze, blows a note on his conch shell and all the little men jump at once.

JUMP in perfect synchronicity, a billion little green men land in the shallow ocean at exactly the same moment. A low bass rumbling groan roars across the ocean, a wave rushes away from the shore and as the wave races away it grows bigger and bigger. The wave continues growing as it flows away, white surf frothing and churning disappearing beyond the horizon and rushing towards the heart of the North American continent.

When Hawaii is swallowed whole the people in California know they are doomed. There are these fools in Las Vegas, who drag their beach chairs onto their lawns and wait for the wave, hoping to be the proud owners of beachfront property. Too bad the wave reaches all the way to Kansas. Las Vegas is obliterated in an instant.

The tsunami is devastating coming in but it is even more destructive going out. As the retreating wall of water recedes, it carries flotsam and jetsam, boulders, trailers, and tractors swirling in the current, debris which scours the earth. Glaciers slowly carved Yosemite, inching along over centuries but this giant wave of Poseidon flooded the mountain range and changed geology in an instant. All those tiny plastic soldiers ride the walls of water like little green surfing superheroes, floating atop the ocean currents to the next invasion point. In the middle of a moonless night the little plastic soldiers gather on the beach and stack themselves into pyramids, all leaping at once and unleashing another tidal wave.

Wave by wave, shore by shore, the little green men invade the world. Poseidon's cavalry leads the charge, plastic toy soldiers saddled atop rubber ducks riding the frothy waves. Poseidon orders his soldiers according to a master plan, changing the directions of the ocean currents, pulverizing the harmonic chord, altering the weather for the entire planet. Using flood, rain, ice, and wave as weapons, Poseidon destroys the world, while I work on my ark, hammer and nail, nail and hammer, board after board. How long is a cubit anyways?

5

My ark floats across an endless ocean. All the continents have disappeared, replaced by chains of archipelagoes. Everything else is ocean, one vast ocean ruled by a crazed oceanographer who calls himself Poseidon and his army of little plastic merman soldiers, floating atop the ocean currents wherever they wish to go. The ark saved my life but I am beginning to think it was not such a good idea. I am so bored. All the ark does is float, we will never be allowed to reach landfall. The little plastic soldiers will make sure of that. So we float and float across a vast and endless ocean.

I tried that Noah trick. You know the one where you release a bird and if it comes back, you are still in the middle of the stinking ocean but if it doesn't then you are near land. The first thirty seven birds I released all came back to the ship but one day, it would have been a Thursday if those things still mattered, one of the birds did not return. The good word spread among the other birds who chattered all night long and then at sunrise took off together in a giant flock. All the birds launched from the ship at once. It was a magnificent sight and I haven't seen any of them since. This was followed by the amphibians hopping off every edge of the ark, landing in the sea with plop after plop. The snakes slithered silently into the sea unseen.

All that was left was the mammals. The only passengers trapped on the ark are me and my fellow mammals. We are loud critters us mammals, roaring, howling, grunting, barking and purring punctuated by the occasional splatter of rumbling flatulence. We mammals are a hairy sweaty smelly bunch. You haven't experienced stink until you have been stuck on a boat with elephant dung, cow pies, horse apples, rabbit pellets, dog doo doo, cat scat, and camel caca. The stench was incredible. Even the skunks were offended.

Two of every animal included me too. I had a wife. Lilith bore me two sons, so the continuation of our species wasn't looking so good. Jonah and Ahab were the apples of my eye. One day a whale swallowed Jonah whole and Ahab took off, swearing vengeance on the white whale. I haven't seen either one since. There was still my wife. Sure we bickered sometimes, bored on the ark, what married couple doesn't bicker, but what could she do about our relationship—I was the last man on earth…

Except I had forgotten about the oceanographer. My wife left me for the mad scientist. So now it is me and the other mammals, floating on an ark in the middle of the ocean. Just floating—floating and stinking.

6

I still remember the day we were saved. I was kneeling on the deck of the ark and praying, begging for a quick and merciful end when a terrible clatter arose in the bathroom. There was a great deal of shrieking and one of the baboons ran out from the tub, towel tied around his waist and his hair all lathered up in shampoo. (The ship had pretty much gone to hell since the night the apes had broken into the bag of forbidden knowledge apples.) The baboon was pretty excited, shrieking, leaping up and down, and baring his teeth in a maniacal grin. He stuck both his monkey hands into his monkey hair and then held his shampoo lathered hands in front of my face. I figured there was probably something wrong with the shampoo. The baboon was pretty vain about his hair. He liked to wear it in a sort of Elvis Presley pompadour. The baboon thought I was some sort of idiot. It wasn't about the hair. It wasn't about the shampoo. It was about the bubbles. The baboon had come up with an idea, a brilliant idea.

We began a bubble factory right there on the ship. I don't want to go into a great deal of detail about manufacturing bubbles except to note that it involved slightly fermenting oats and plenty of zebra flatulence. Messy, nasty stuff, zebra farts and on an ark full of hairy smelly mammals that is saying something. The bubbles surface was made of a sticky glue. We made a gazillion bubbles and set them free to float atop the ocean, drifting all across the world. Imagine the sight at sunrise of millions and millions of bubbles floating away from the ark, bubble skin glinting in the dawn.

The rubber ducks did not like the stinky sticky bubbles. The rubber ducks migrated. Who knew rubber ducks could fly, but as the ocean became polluted with millions of sticky bubbles, the rubber ducks suddenly rose up from the water all at once, flapping their little yellow wings frenetically and then the rubber ducks flew away.

Gradually all of Poseidon's floating army of little plastic soldiers got stuck to the bubbles and got stuck to each other. One day my ex-wife returned. Lilith was stuck to a thousand different little plastic soldiers. I threw her back to the sea, not realizing that she would return again and again. One by one, all the little plastic soldiers became stuck to each other and the sticky bubbles. Poseidon was defeated.

As ocean levels fall and the archipelagos swell back into continents they are not exactly the same. The bugs and reptiles no longer respect us. I do not think it will be easy for mammals to become the top of the food chain again. So I am not certain if being saved from the cruel reign of Poseidon has been such a good thing.

For one thing the baboon is now boss. Ever since the baboon invented the bubble machines and led the revolution to overthrow the tyrant Poseidon, the other mammals on the ark demanded that the baboon be put in charge and I was demoted. The baboon lords it over me pretty good. He calls me his "banana boy". After the fall of Poseidon, my ex-wife left the oceanographer and now Lilith dates the baboon. She says it's the hair, "drives her wild." The sounds of their vigorous monkey love fill the boat. "If the ark is a rocking don't bother knocking."

7

Without the little plastic army men floating atop the sea, the ark is free to travel from archipelago to archipelago. As we travel from island to island different species leave the ark. The hippopotamus were the first to depart, dropping off at an island with beautiful lagoons and plenty of aquatic weeds. The giraffes and gazelles were left off at long sandy beaches with plenty of room to run. The skunks and ferrets looked like their island was the most fun. They built wonderful waterslides, frolicking all day long.

At last we discovered a small island which held surviving humans. Before the Poseidon Wars the island had been a top secret government installation. It had been atop a mountain in Wyoming but rising ocean levels had left only the peak poking above the endless ocean. The little island was filled with government scientists, military personnel, and a handful of lawyers. I had the ark drop me off at the island of the humans. Lilith stayed on the ark, waving goodbye to me as she floated away, holding hands with the bubble inventing baboon wearing the handsome Elvis Presley pompadour.

There was a lot of bickering on the island of the humans. The government scientists conducted a study. The study discovered that the bickering was caused by the lawyers. The military personnel were assigned the task of killing the lawyers. It wasn't hard. Some of the military personnel seemed to enjoy it. Luckily, before they became extinct, we decided to keep a few lawyers around just in case they served a necessary purpose in our tiny little human ecosystem. Between the scientists, soldiers, and lawyers, I am probably the dumbest person on the island. I am still known as "banana boy."

The scientists are beginning to rebuild our civilization and technology. Not exactly the same technology and civilization, but a new society adapted to this strange brave new world. In many ways it is an island paradise. No traffic, no smog, no crime, and only a handful of lawyers. We have food, shelter, and the weather is warm enough to remove the need for clothing. Not surprisingly, on an island full of naked people the fertility rate skyrockets.

8

You have to wonder what comes next. I ponder the future, walking along the shore. I always find that walking beside the ocean is a wonderful way to think. My footsteps fall into time with the rhythmic crashing of the surf upon the sand. I have no idea where I am. Not that it matters, because if I have learned anything through all these adventures it is this: no matter where you go, there you are. This place used to have a name but that doesn't matter anymore. This place will probably have another name somewhere in the future but that doesn't matter either. This is just where I am at this moment, walking beside the ocean and thinking my thoughts. Not that I am thinking deep thoughts or getting close to figuring things out, mostly I am just trying to survive. So in many ways, despite everything that has happened and how everything has changed, really nothing has changed. I am still just trying to survive. Just like before.

The next wave which washes upon the shore brings with it a gift, a tennis shoe surfing atop the white froth and skidding to a stop on the sand. Except for being soggy and wet the tennis shoe seems perfectly fine. This tennis shoe has floated atop the ocean currents for years, surviving the tsunamis, and even surviving the sea monsters unleashed by Poseidon.

That is one tough shoe.

The shoe is an 8 1\2—just my size. I slip the shoe on my left foot. It fits comfortably. It looks good. Then I resume walking along the shore, leaving behind a pair of unmatched footprints in the sand, one set of tracks civilized and shod, the other footprints barbaric and barefoot, and all traces of my path wiped away by the crashing of the waves eventually.

గ్ర

Gary Every *is a four time nominee for the Rhysling Award, and the author of two novellas;* Inca Butterflies *from Hadrosaur Productions and* The Saint and The Robot *from Sam's Dot Publishing. His science fiction appears in magazines such as* Tales of the Talisman, Starline, Dreams and Nightmares *and many more. An anthology of the best of his award winning newspaper columns about Arizona history, folkore, Native Americans, and environment, titled* Shadow of the OhshaD *is available from Amazon.com.*